BRIDE OF THE TOWER

SHARON SCHULZE

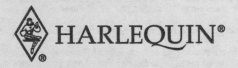

HARLEQUIN®

TORONTO • NEW YORK • LONDON
AMSTERDAM • PARIS • SYDNEY • HAMBURG
STOCKHOLM • ATHENS • TOKYO • MILAN • MADRID
PRAGUE • WARSAW • BUDAPEST • AUCKLAND

Special thanks and acknowledgment
are given to Elizabeth Bailey for her contribution
to THE STEEPWOOD SCANDAL series.

ISBN 0-373-29250-3

BRIDE OF THE TOWER

Please address questions and book requests to:
Harlequin Reader Service
U.S.: 3010 Walden Ave., P.O. Box 1325, Buffalo, NY 14269
Canadian: P.O. Box 609, Fort Erie, Ont. L2A 5X3

To Linda Harmon, Leslie O'Grady and Joyce C. Ware—
critique partners and friends extraordinaire.

And to my wonderful editor, Melissa Endlich,
with many thanks for her patience and encouragement.

Chapter One

Sherwood Forest, Nottinghamshire, 1217

Sir William Bowman glanced back at the big black gelding lagging along behind him. Bran had come up lame soon after they'd entered the forest, but they couldn't stop yet. Pausing to stroke the horse's swollen fetlock, Will murmured soothing words rather than the curses echoing through his head, gave a gentle tug on the reins and picked up his stride.

The sun disappeared behind the tall trees, leaving naught but an eerie yellow glow that made specters of the branches overhanging the narrow path. Will peered into the deepening gloom. Not true night, but close enough to warn him he'd best find shelter soon. Like a fool, he'd allowed his anger to distract him; he'd already wandered so deep into the dense forest he wondered if he'd e'er find his way out again.

He and Bran had roamed far in Lord Rannulf's service these past weeks, a long journey nowhere near finished. What he wouldn't give for a flask of usquebaugh and the company of a warm and willing maid at the end of this part of it! Yet thanks to Sir Richard Belleville's overcautious nature, Will now found himself lost in Nottingham forest with an injured mount instead of lodged comfortably at the next keep along his way, where he'd planned to spend the night.

Damn Sir Richard! He'd kept Will so occupied with trivialities that he'd had no chance to leave Birkland—surely the least important of Lord Rannulf's keeps—until well after the midday meal. Yet when Will had suggested he wait until the next morn to resume his travels, the slippery knave had nigh slammed the gates behind Will himself!

And in their haste to see Will escorted on his way, it seemed Sir Richard's men had set Will upon the wrong path through the forest, for 'twas clear this route had seen little traffic of late.

Nor did it appear to lead anywhere but deeper into the wilderness of Sherwood.

He could do naught to remedy that mistake tonight, alas. He'd be better served instead to calm his anger and use the sense God gave him to find his way out of this dilemma.

Assuming, of course, that he had any sense. His low chuckle sounded loud in the silent woods. Judging by his recent behavior, that seemed doubtful. He squared his shoulders and buried deep the lingering sense of imminent threat that skittered down his spine. He was a knight well blooded in his lord's service, he reminded himself sternly, not some cringing villain afraid of shadows and looming dark.

Bran nudged him in the back as though to urge him to move faster and crept up nigh onto Will's heels. Had the gelding with his better hearing noticed something he could not? Will shifted the reins to his left hand and hitched his sword into a more accessible position with his right. Best to be prepared.

At least the outlaws of years past were no more—a blessing, no doubt, though the thought of spending time with their legendary band held a tantalizing appeal. Tales of Robin of the Hood had traveled even into the remote area of the Marches where l'Eau Clair Keep stood guard over the Welsh border. As a youth, Will had been fascinated by the stories; time and again he and his compatriots had roamed the rugged countryside in search of adventures, taking it in turn to be part of the band of outlaws or the sheriff's henchmen.

A flock of birds shot up out of the brush, startling him from his memories and sending Bran into a squealing, plunging frenzy. Teeth bared and ears pressed flat, the gelding reared back, dragging Will along with him. "Easy, lad," Will crooned, grabbing at the slippery leather as the reins slipped through his gloved hand and his feet slid through the loose leaves covering the ground. By the rood, he'd ne'er seen Bran react so sharply to so little provocation!

Wanting to free his sword hand to hold the bucking beast, Will tried to shove his sword into the scabbard one-handed, but another bird swooped close overhead. Bran jerked back hard. Off balance, Will tumbled backward into a prickly thicket as the terrified gelding, eyes rolling wildly, somehow spun around on the narrow path and raced off the way they'd come.

The uneven clatter of hoofbeats echoed away.

Cursing in a mixture of Welsh, English and Norman French—which didn't relieve his frustration a whit—Will fought the clinging brambles and twisted free of the thick brush. *Jesu,* 'twas a miracle he hadn't impaled himself on his own blade!

He wrenched his sword belt around and rammed the weapon home, plucking thorns and leaves from his surcoat. He could only be glad he'd been wearing his mail, for other than a few scratches on his cheek, he'd emerged unscathed. But Bran had disappeared into the night, carrying with him all of Will's baggage save the small pack he carried slung over one shoulder.

He'd best go after the beast at once, before it got too dark to follow him. It would do neither of them any good for the horse to injure himself further, nor for them to blunder deeper into the wood.

Will stood for a moment and let his eyes adjust to the deepening gloom, all his attention focused on the silence surrounding him. No sound or glimpse of light pierced the trees to give him a hint of civilization nearby, or a clue to which direction Bran had headed. Giving a weary sigh, Will shifted his pack higher on his shoulder and set off along the faint trail through the heavy brush.

How far could the beast have gone, after all, injured as he was? Besides, there was no place to settle for the night here. Perhaps he could find his way back to Birkland—no doubt Bran's destination, he thought wryly.

Though he doubted whether Sir Richard would allow him—or his horse—to spend another night within the confines of Birkland. He'd certainly been in a hurry to see them gone.

By the time Will stumbled from the heavy forest onto a rutted road, the moon had risen high in the sky and he felt ready to sleep on the first clear bit of ground he could find. Of his errant mount, he'd found no sign save a few broken branches far back on the path near where the horse had taken off. He could only hope he'd find the horse's trail more easily come morning. For now, however, since the road before him looked well-traveled, he might as well follow it. It had to lead somewhere.

A rustle of sound made him pause. Leaves fell down from the branches overhead, heralding the two men who leapt into the path in front of Will before his sword had cleared the scabbard. Faces masked, weapons raised, they set upon him at once.

Will drew a long-bladed dagger from his boot with his free hand and laid about him with a vengeance. 'Twas hard to follow his opponents in the shifting moon shadows, but he'd been alert before the attack, his senses focused wide about him. He used that intensity now to gauge what they would do.

They could not see him well, either, thankfully, for 'twas soon apparent they were skilled fighters. Will parried blows and thrust at the pair with some success, judging from their grunts and cries of pain, though not without sustaining a few injuries of his own.

Warm blood trickled down his brow and arm as he began to flag. He cried out a few breathless taunts, hoping to draw them into foolishness, but 'twas a waste of time. They seemed tireless, and with two of them against him alone, he began to wonder if perhaps he could not outlast them after all.

A blade slid over the mail covering his shoulder and slipped down his throat. The sharp pain spurred him on, even as his foes redoubled their efforts, as well. A hard blow to the head sent Will reeling, and they were upon him like flies to a midden, pummeling him, knocking loose his weapons and moving in for the kill. A stream of blood gushed from his forehead and ran into his eyes, further blurring his vision.

A hard pounding sounded in the distance, drowning out the heavy pulse of his heartbeat. He could scarce care about its cause when he couldn't find the strength to hold himself upright. He clung to his knife—a meager defense, but better than nothing—as his legs crumpled beneath him and he muttered a silent prayer that his death be swift and clean.

But before his attackers could strike a killing blow, the distant sound became the thunder of hoofbeats drawing near. Muttering curses, the two men turned and fled into the forest, leaving Will sprawled in the road.

He tried to stand, but could not make his legs support him. His searching fingers closed about the hilt of his sword and he dragged it close as the horses came to a plunging halt nigh at his feet.

Had he survived the attack to be run down in the road instead? He pulled himself up on one elbow and stared at the blurred, shifting scene before him, but he could make no sense of it. Horses shuffled their feet nearby, appearing, to his bleary gaze, to have too many legs and heads; moonlight shimmered eerily on the armed and mail-clad riders, lending them an otherworldly appearance. One of them called another "milady."

Were they the warrior women of legend, come to escort him to Valhalla? Or the devil's hand-maidens, mayhap, ready to carry him away to Hell? Did it matter? Will tried to laugh, but 'twas a feeble attempt. Whoever they were, if he must spend eternity with them, he hoped they were beautiful.

Perhaps he hadn't survived after all, Will thought as he watched the smallest of the riders slip from the saddle and remove his helmet. For unless the blow to his head had scrambled his brain completely, 'twas a flesh-and-blood woman who dropped to her knees at Will's side and leaned down to touch his face. "Rest easy, sir, and let us help you," she murmured as she shifted and reached down beside him. Before Will could reply or give in to the urge to resist, she slid his sword from his grasp and handed it to a man behind her.

Disarmed by a woman again! Will's confusion mounted as his vision began to fade. Her long, disheveled braid brushed over his face, teasing his senses with the scent of flowers. Unfamiliar, but clearly a woman—not Gillian, however.

But who was she? He squinted up at her, but her features blurred in the uneven light. His strength gone, his arm collapsed beneath him. His head hit the ground, and he knew no more.

"Hellfire, he's swooned." Lady Julianna d'Arcy grabbed hold of the fallen man's mail-clad arm—caught beneath him when he collapsed— and shifted it to rest at his side. Her touch gentle, she brushed his hair away from his brow with a frown. Blood welled under her fingers and ran down his face; more dark streaks of it oozed sluggishly from his neck and arm.

He clearly needed more help than she could give him here. She grabbed the hem of her surcoat and sliced away two strips of fabric with the long dagger lying beside him on the road. "Rolf, come help me bind his wounds, then you and Bart may move him."

Bart knelt on the far side of the victim and carefully raised the man so she could wind the material round his brow while Rolf tended to his throat. "Move him where, milady?" Bart asked.

She knotted the linen and used the end of it to blot away the worst of the blood besmirching the man's face. "Back to Tuck's Tower, of course." Clambering to her feet, she took up the dagger and thrust it into her boot top, next to her own.

"Bring a stranger within our walls, milady?" Bart protested as he rose.

"He's no danger to anyone in his present condition," Julianna pointed out tartly. By the saints, would he ever cease to look upon her as a child? Her father had been gone for nigh on a year now, her mother slightly more, yet unlike most of her people, Bart continued to quietly challenge her authority to rule her lands, treating her instead as the cherished young lady of Tuck's Tower.

Something she'd never sought to be—and had certainly never been.

Rolf, waiting patiently near the injured man's head, motioned for Bart to help lift him, but her father's old retainer ignored him and moved closer to Julianna. "What of later, Lady Julianna?" he asked low-voiced. "Once he's healed? What will you do then, if he turns out to be dangerous?"

"You dare to question me, Bart—to question me here, now?" Though she kept her tone as re-

strained as Bart's, she made certain he could not
mistake her displeasure. "Make no mistake, we
shall discuss this later." Biting back a snarl of
frustration, Julianna spun away and bent to grasp
the victim's feet. She nodded to Rolf and they
lifted the man. "Now is hardly the time," she
added. "At this point, the poor fool's more like
to die here in the road."

Though 'twas a struggle for her—the fellow
was tall and solidly built—she didn't permit herself so much as a grunt of discomfort as they carried him to her mount.

"I'll take him with me," she said, gratefully
shifting her burden to a glowering Bart and climbing unassisted onto her mount.

It took three men, grumbling and complaining,
to support the fellow and shift him into the saddle
before her. Biting back a few curses of her own,
Julianna fitted her arms about him to hold him
more securely. His tall, lean body fit snug against
her, his back to her front, making her all too
aware of his muscled physique even through the
layers of mail separating them.

She eased her hold a bit, making him groan and
shift in her grasp and his empty scabbard bump
against her leg. Tightening her hold again, she

glanced about, hoping to catch a glimpse of his sword. If he survived, he'd not thank her for leaving the weapon behind in the forest.

And if he did not, 'twould be another blade to add to her own ever-dwindling arsenal. Though the thought made her feel like a grave robber, of late she'd reached the point where she could not afford to be too particular. As long as she wasn't forced to turn outlaw…

"Rolf, find his sword and anything else that looks like it belongs to him," she ordered. "His horse, as well, if it hasn't run off. God willing, he'll have need of them someday soon."

Wheeling her mount, she led her troop along the moon-shadowed trail, doing her best to ignore the intriguing feel of the man's weight pressing her into the saddle. She glanced down at the stranger's face, at the strength no amount of blood and bruising could hide.

And prayed she'd not have cause to regret this night's work.

Chapter Two

The torches along the walls of Tuck's Tower glowed in the distance, a welcome greeting that lent Julianna the strength to hold on to the man slumped in her arms a bit longer. Never had the road from the forest to the keep seemed so long, nor her own resources so puny. She'd worked hard to perfect the ability to suppress any signs of exhaustion or weakness, yet this unknown man threatened to expose the woman she tried to hide beneath her mannish ways.

The weight of him, his muscled body nested against her, felt foreign in a deliciously intriguing way, making her aware of how different her own body was from his. Tall and lean, *male*. The scent of leather and armor, the subtle brush of his whiskered cheek against her neck…. That simple contact heightened her senses until her mind and body fair reeled from the overwhelming enticement of sound, scent and touch.

But the tide of heat that passed through her owed as much to embarrassment as to feminine awareness. To feel such things for a man nigh lifeless in her arms! What was wrong with her? Had she grown so desperate in her self-imposed chastity?

She shook her head in disgust. 'Twas an easy thing to live a chaste life when not faced with temptation. The good Lord knew she'd never before been tempted by any man at Tuck's Tower.

Or elsewhere.

'Twas a good thing she had not, she thought wryly as she rode beneath the raised portcullis and nudged her mount toward the stables. For if she were to give herself to a man, she suspected her fragile and treasured authority over Tuck's Tower and all who dwelled within its walls would come to an end.

And that, she would never allow to happen— not while she had breath in her body, and the support of her doting and powerful uncle—her overlord—behind her.

She'd willingly sacrifice herself for Tuck's Tower, if need be.

Two of her men approached and eased the wounded man from her grasp, though she feared she'd not free herself of the feelings he'd engendered within her so readily. But she'd work to do it now, to settle the man and treat his injuries. For the sooner he recovered and left Tuck's Tower, the less opportunity for her to do something she might regret.

Despite the late hour and her own state of exhaustion, Julianna took charge of seeing to her unexpected guest. The fact that outsiders seldom passed through their gates had made some of her people suspicious of every stranger, while others—mostly those too young to realize the threat a stranger could pose—would welcome anyone to Tuck's Tower without a thought of caution. Julianna, however, had been taught vigilance nigh from the cradle; she would protect her own until time and experience allowed her to do otherwise.

They carried the man to a small chamber adjoining hers—a room equipped with stout doors that could be locked—and laid him upon a straw pallet on the floor. After she'd given them several low-voiced commands, the men-at-arms left.

Biting back a sigh of exhaustion, Julianna entered her chamber and collected the night candle from beside her bed, kindled it and returned to the storeroom to set the tall iron stand next to her patient. The thick taper cast its brightness too high to be of much use, although it gave her a clear enough look at him to see that the disheveled hair hanging to his shoulders, where not matted with blood, was dark blond.

Bending over him, she adjusted the makeshift bandage wound tightly about his brow. "You are a handsome one," she murmured, then shook her head in disgust at her weakness. "Though that matters not a whit."

She went back to her room to collect more candles and water. "Who are you?" she mused. "And what were you doing in Sherwood on foot, all alone?"

If he survived his injuries, she'd learn those answers as soon as he could speak, for she scarce dared trust anyone anymore, even those she knew. Strangers—especially well-armed strangers— posed far too great a risk. She refused to permit anyone or anything to threaten her tenuous control over Tuck's Tower, for she dared not risk losing all she held dear.

However, of late her nerves and resources had been stretched to the limit. If her uncle knew about the recent chaos and suspicious events in the area, he might decide to remove control of Tuck's Tower from her hands, make it but another minor holding in his succession of manors and keeps spread about the land. He might also decide to carry her off to court or to live with him and his family—to live a noble lady's life, to be wed to a stranger, to be forced to live someplace far from her home.

The ewer, which should have been full, stood nigh empty, and the candle stubs in the holder from the table were too short to be of use. Another example of recent events; with most of the servants pressed into service for defense and other tasks, many of the usual household chores had fallen by the wayside. She poured the dregs from the pitcher onto a washrag, then stuck her head out into the narrow corridor and shouted for someone to bring more candles, hot water, her box of simples and a maid skilled in healing.

Unwilling to leave her patient alone any longer, she snatched a branch of candles from the table by the hearth, pausing at the sound of heavy footsteps outside the chamber.

"My lady." Rolf stood in the doorway, her basket of medicines clutched to his brawny chest. "Thought you might need me for something."

"Aye." She set aside the cloth and candles from her chamber, arranging them on the floor alongside the pallet. "Help me out of this armor, if you would." She'd a long night ahead of her, with naught but her own will to overcome her exhaustion. Though the mail hauberk and leggings allowed her to move freely, they weighed heavy upon her after a day's wear, and they made kneeling for any length of time uncomfortable.

She bent at the waist and gave a groan of relief as Rolf assisted her in drawing the hauberk over her head. She left the armor where it fell and turned away to tug off her boots, then unbuckled the straps at the waist of the mail leggings and slid them off. Her padded undertunic and linen leggings, uncomfortably damp with sweat, clung to her skin, but she would wait until after she took care of her guest—her prisoner?—to change out of them.

Stretching and rolling her shoulders did little to ease the tension holding her within its grip, but her own discomfort mattered little compared to her unknown patient's wounds. Instead, she pulled off her undertunic and tugged her shirttail loose, rolled up her sleeves and, taking up the candles, lighted them to brighten the small chamber.

Dropping to her knees beside the pallet, she motioned for Rolf to help her remove the stranger's blood-stained armor. 'Twas much more difficult to free him from his mail than it had been for her to slip out of her own, since he could not stand or help in any way. His wounds made the task nigh impossible. By the time they'd stripped him to his undertunic and braes, while trying to protect his injuries and the makeshift bandages covering them, Julianna was drenched with sweat and felt as though she'd just wrestled an ox into submission.

Blotting her forehead on her sleeve, she settled down beside the still-unconscious man, wincing as her leggings caught on the rough floor boards. She yanked out the large splinter jabbing her backside and muttered a curse, though she wished she could howl out her pain and frustration instead. She was hungry, weary and sore—none of which was likely to change for the better anytime soon—and the servants and supplies she'd called for were nowhere in sight.

Shifting to a more comfortable position, Julianna took up a cloth and wet it, dabbing at the blood covering the man's brow. He immediately began to shift about and moan. Had she been too rough? Mayhap she was not the best person to care for him. She laid her hand on his shoulder to quiet him and glanced up at Rolf. "Go get Mary—" A sound outside the door made her pause, but 'twas only two maidservants with the water and candles she'd requested. Julianna sat back on her heels and swiped her sleeve absently over her damp face yet again while the girls carried in a bucket, a basin and two short, fat candles. "Bring her to me at once."

"Aye, milady." Rolf followed the servants to the door, pausing when Julianna called his name.

"Look in the barracks first," she told him, not bothering to disguise her displeasure. "If you find her there, I want to know about it. I cannot have her stirring the men to fight each other over her favors yet again. If they're foolish enough to do so, 'twould normally be their business, but we cannot spare anyone at the moment. Our safety is far more important than their lust."

Though Rolf's expression didn't change, Julianna could see from the look in his eyes that

he'd keep Mary away from the barracks one way
or another. At this point, she thought wearily, she
didn't much care how he did it. If they hadn't
needed Mary's skills as a healer, Julianna would
have sent the round-heeled wench on her way
long since.

"Don't you worry none, milady. I'll see to it."
He nodded respectfully and left.

The door had no sooner closed behind Rolf
than her patient began to stir. Eyes open wide, he
stared up at her, his gaze unfocused and his face
twisted into a grimace of pain. "Poor man," Julianna murmured. "I'll give you a draught to ease
you soon." She bent over him, smoothing her
hand over his brow and shifting sweat- and blood-
matted hair away from the large bump above his
temple. A bit lower and he'd likely have died
from the blow. She could do little to treat that
injury save clean it, but she'd do what she could
for the others.

She drew her hand down his cheek and along
his jaw in a soothing caress, frowning as her callused fingers scraped against his whiskers. 'Twas
not a lady's smooth hand, she reminded herself,
but 'twas competent enough to save him, whether
it be with sword or simples.

And if she were to care for his wounds, it seemed she'd have to do so without any other help. Giving his face one last stroke, she shifted to get to her feet, then let out a shriek when he clamped his hand hard about her wrist.

"What—" His voice, barely audible despite her nearness, faded away. Licking at his lips, he tugged on her arm and drew Julianna closer. He drew a deep breath and squinted up at her, his blue eyes intense. "What is this place? Is it Birkland?"

Julianna covered his hand and loosened his hold on her wrist, her mind awhirl. Birkland. Could he be one of Richard's men? There was nothing familiar about him or his garb, but she'd heard rumors that Richard had hired mercenaries to shore up Birkland's defenses and help him in his quest for power.

By the Virgin, *had* she brought an enemy within their walls?

His fingers relaxed within her grasp and, moaning, he closed his eyes and slumped onto the pallet. She laid his hand on his chest and sat back on her heels. Enemy or not, he posed no threat at the moment, nor would he in the future, she vowed, for she'd keep him under close guard at all times.

For now, however, she'd more work ahead of her, for she could wait no longer for Mary to arrive. No doubt the wench was the worse for drink again, and would be no use to anyone. Deciding to deal with her later, Julianna poured water into the basin, then reached for her basket of simples.

Shifting the candles for better light, she cast the man one last look. *Please don't be an enemy,* she pleaded silently, though she knew in her heart that it mattered not a whit whether he was friend or foe. Now that she'd held him close within her arms, felt the warmth and weight of him against her skin, he'd become real to her—not some anonymous stranger she might wield her sword against in battle.

Her hands steady, she stared at his motionless face and said a swift prayer for guidance as she stripped off the first bandage and began to wash blood away from the wound.

She sent up another plea, as well—that her intuition had not misled her.

For no matter who this man might be, she could not let him die.

* * *

Julianna quietly closed the door to her chamber and slumped back against the well-worn planks with a sigh of bone-deep weariness. Though she'd had a brief chance to rest her body once she'd settled the wounded stranger in the chamber beside her own, her mind hadn't allowed her a moment's respite as it circled round and round the dilemma of his identity and his reason for being so near Tuck's Tower.

Once Rolf had returned—bearing the news that Mary would be of no use to anyone this night, for she lay in the barracks in a drunken stupor—she'd asked him to watch over the man, for she'd duties aplenty yet to see to before she could return to her chambers.

Now that her tasks were done, she'd still have no chance to seek her bed before another day passed. She couldn't ask poor Rolf to stay up the whole night, not when he'd been on guard duty at the gate all the night before with no rest in between. She needed her good fighters as alert and ready as possible.

As for herself, she'd managed on little sleep many times before. If her patient slumbered through the night, perhaps she could snatch a nap. If not, 'twas a sacrifice she'd gladly make, for to give of herself in any way she must was a part of her responsibility to Tuck's Tower and its inhabitants. Despite the man's injuries, she dared not leave him unguarded.

Before she sent Rolf away, however, she'd take a moment to avail herself of the basin of warm water awaiting her on the hearth and the clean garb hanging on a hook nearby.

Julianna pushed away from the door, set the bar across to lock it, and took up the night candle beside the bed, lighting the candles near the low fire before stripping off her sweat-stained shirt and braes. Stifling a yawn, she stretched her tired shoulders, wincing at the tightness she felt from the unaccustomed task of holding a man's dead weight before her in the saddle. At least, praise the Virgin, he was not dead in truth.

Nor had she harmed him with her rudimentary treatment of his wounds, she hoped, sending another brief prayer heavenward.

She unwound the cloth binding her breasts and tossed aside the long strip of linen with a sigh of pure pleasure, for she'd not need to wear it again till the morn. Naked, she sank down on the drying cloth spread out on the hearthstones to let the fire's warmth soak into her aching body and took up the small, precious piece of soap from beside the basin.

The clean scent of flowers made her smile, for as always, it brought her mother to mind. Whether dressed in a fine embroidered gown or her husband's cast-off garments, Lady Marian d'Arcy had appeared a lady, and had always smelled of sweet summer blooms blended with spices from the East. She had mixed the scent herself. 'Twas as unique and precious as the woman who'd worn it, Julianna thought, and as unforgettable.

She regretted now that she'd not paid more attention when her mother sought to pass the skill on to her, for her supply of the soap and perfume was dwindling and she wasn't sure she'd the knowledge—or the time, if truth be told—to replenish it. 'Twas a luxury she could live without, most likely, of a certainty less important than ensuring her troops were well-trained and the keep's inhabitants fed and cared for.

She brought the soap to her nose and savored its fragrance once more before dipping it into the basin and rubbing it into the washrag. Though she nearly always dressed in men's garb—indeed, she could scarce recall the last time she'd worn anything else—for now she'd take what womanly pleasure she could from the fruits of her mother's ability by perfuming her body with the fragrance of flowers.

She closed her eyes and fought back tears as she imagined that the cloud of scent enveloping her came from her mother's arms wrapped warm and tight about her. If only her mother were here with her now, to share her wise counsel about so many things! Instead, Julianna hummed a tune her mother often sang and sought comfort from her memories as she washed herself from head to toe, dressed and brushed out her hair.

The words of the song made her blush when she recalled them, for they told of a woman readying herself to meet her lover. The handsome blond stranger filled her thoughts until, with a moan of self-disgust, she pushed his unsettling image from her mind. The fact that there might be another reason altogether for her to take such care with her appearance made her blush all the more. 'Twas naught but a simple need to be clean and comfortable, she told herself, that had her bathing in the middle of the night; it had nothing to do with the man who lay sleeping but a short distance away.

The man she'd keep watch over for the rest of the night.

"Blessed Virgin, save me from myself," she whispered, "for 'tis clear I've something wrong with me! Never before have I met a man who could make me doubt my own strength of will." She tossed her loosened hair back over her shoulders. "I'd be a fool, indeed, to allow this stranger to tempt me in any way."

Her determination fixed, she squared her shoulders, left her chamber and went to send Rolf off to bed.

Flickering candlelight and a low-voiced moan woke Julianna from a restless sleep. She forced her eyes open in time to see her patient attempting to sit up and nearly toppling a lighted branch of candles. Since she'd drifted off sitting propped against the wall, she shifted to her knees and caught him by the shoulders, clasping him against her as she rolled them away from the wavering flames. "Have a care," she warned, "else you'll set the place afire." The words trailed to a whisper as they came to rest with him atop her, his weight pressing the air from her lungs.

He lay motionless atop her, his eyes squeezed

shut and his breath gusting hard near her ear. He felt heavier than she'd imagined he'd be, his body relaxed upon hers, his muscular frame molded against her as though they were meant to fit together. She couldn't tell if he'd swooned, or was simply unable to move, but either way she hesitated to push him off her, for she was sure 'twould cause him further harm.

Yet she dared not remain in this position, either, for it felt too good, too enticing...too likely to tempt her to foolishness. Fighting back the sensation, she tried to squirm out from under him, to no avail. He held her pinned fast to the floor—rough splintery oak beneath her, warm temptation above.

"Do I know you well enough for us to be doing this?" he whispered into Julianna's hair, bringing her wriggling to a swift halt.

She stared up into his eyes, dark blue and surprisingly full of amusement, and tried to draw a deep breath to steady her suddenly racing pulse. Even if she'd had air enough to speak, she knew not what she'd have said, for he held her captive with both his body and his warm gaze.

Mesmerized, Julianna returned his stare and waited.

Chapter Three

William sank down against the lissome woman who had, unfortunately, ceased her provocative movements beneath him, and buried his face in her hair while he gathered his strength. By the rood! The way his head throbbed and his stomach roiled, he must have fair climbed inside an ale barrel last night.

'Twas a shame he couldn't remember anything, for his body was most pleased indeed by the woman beneath him. He drew in a deep breath and sought to settle himself. 'Twould not do to lose the battle and swoon—or worse—over his bedmate.

She didn't have the feel of his usual choice— short, buxom and well-padded. She fit perfectly against him, though, nigh tall enough to reach his

shoulder when they stood, he'd guess, and her
body's gentle curves all the more stimulating
against him for the lack of excessive flesh. He
nestled atop her with a sigh and rested his aching
head on the soft mass of dark, wavy hair cascad-
ing over her shoulder. Ah, this was satisfaction
indeed! Why had he never before realized the al-
lure of a strong, slim woman?

He drew in another deep breath to clear his
muddled brain and smiled his pleasure as his
lungs filled with the beguiling scent of woman, of
flowers and spice, firing his blood hotter still. She
must be far cleaner than the usual tavern wench
as well; he'd not smelled such a wonderful fragrance since he'd last visited Gillian's solar at
l'Eau Clair.

The realization shot through him as sharply as
an arrow—he could not mistake the sweet perfume of a noble lady.

A noble lady...

Christ on the Cross, what had he done?

Arms stiffening, Will levered himself up and
tried to climb off her, sending a lightning bolt of
agony through his head and arm, while the pulsing pain in his neck killed the throb of pleasure

in his loins as effectively as a cold shower of water.

She moved at the same time, giving him a shove that pushed him over and off her. He slammed to the floor on his back and stayed where he'd landed, his vision fading in and out and a wave of dizziness making his stomach threaten to rebel. Will sprawled before the woman like a drunkard, unable to so much as sit up. The impact sent shards of pain through his neck and arm, as well, reminding him exactly how he'd come to this pass.

'Twas not too much ale that had brought him here, wherever "here" was.

Cursing beneath her breath, Julianna scrambled to her knees beside the man. His quiet moans of pain, as well as the solid thump of his body as it hit the hard oak planks, sent a wave of guilt through her. He lay so still, she wondered if she'd knocked him senseless.

She ran a soothing hand over his face, smoothing the hair back from his brow, and reached for the wet cloth draped over the bowl of water. Guilt tinged with regret, she admitted to herself as she eased the cloth across his bandaged forehead. Those few, brief moments of his weight atop her, his hard lean body obviously responding to the feel of a woman beneath him, had sent a shard of pleasure shooting through her before her years of training had jolted to life and she'd thrown him off.

She'd grown so used to fighting back at any physical contact—not that she'd ever before experienced anything like *that*—that her body responded as a warrior, not a woman.

Though why she should react with such intense lust to the inadvertent touch of a complete stranger shocked her nigh as much as the realization that she wished it would happen again....

With her patient awake and aware of *her,* of Julianna—not simply responding to a warm female body beneath his.

What else could account for his reaction? He knew no more of her than she did of him.

He pushed aside the damp rag, caught her hand in a surprisingly solid grip and squinted up at her. "Who are you?" he asked, demand lacing his voice despite its quiet tone.

"Hush." She slipped her fingers free of his and reached to pick up the cloth from where it had fallen on the floor. "You must rest, sir. Who I am matters not a whit."

His arms shook as he levered himself into a half-sitting position, then, his face nigh as pale as the linen swathed about his brow, settled his back against the wall. "I fear it does, mistress—" He caught hold of her hair and let it sift through his fingers, then tightened his grasp and raised the disheveled locks to his face and inhaled deeply. He glanced up at her. "Or should I call you 'milady'?" His tone matched his gaze—sharp, measuring.

Challenging.

And she'd always loved a challenge.

A silent voice inside her brain warred with the soft, yearning part of her that wanted to inch closer to him, to tempt fate.

To tempt *him.*

Yet her good sense warned her to beware this intriguing man despite the way her senses fought to cease all thought—to feel, to react, to follow the instinctual draw of his body to her own.

Sound reasoning won out, and she gathered her hair in her hand to free it. "You need not call me anything at all," she snarled.

Rather than release her, however, he wound her hair about his hand until his knuckles pressed against hers and she was forced to shift nearer to him else she'd fall. His breath whispered against her cheek, warm, distracting. "But I must," he insisted, his voice low, rough, intimate. He gazed at her with undisguised heat. "Considering how close we've been." He leaned closer still and brushed his lips over hers. "And are like to become."

The insinuation coloring his voice—or was it the feel of his mouth upon hers?—sent a wave of heat through her body and a fiery flush to her cheeks. She mentally shook herself free of his spell and drew a deep breath. "That is most unlikely, sir, I assure you." Heedless of whether or not she lost a hank of hair, Julianna wrapped her free hand about his to pry loose his fingers and jerked away from him, just as he released his hold. She fell sideways to the floor, barely avoiding the candle stand as she rolled clear, becoming tangled in her tousled cloud of hair in the process.

He slipped back against the wall with a thump.

"By the Virgin, you're an insolent knave." She thrust her hands through her hair, pushed it away from her face and scrambled to her feet, moving to stand over him. "I've a mind to send you down to the cellars to recover," she added as she flung her hair back over her shoulder and bent to peer at him.

He didn't groan this time, nor make any response at all to her threat. He lay slumped against the wall, his head lolled to the side and his face contorted with pain. The fury drained from her and she dropped to her knees beside him. A nudge at his shoulder produced no reaction from him, instead sending him sliding bonelessly toward the floor.

Catching hold of him, she bit back a curse and lowered him onto his pallet. He remained quiet, and he made no move to help or to resist her as she moved him into a more comfortable position.

Julianna shifted to sit beside him. "Dear God, have I killed him?" She touched the side of his neck and felt his lifeblood pulsing strong against her fingers. At least he still lived, though considering his treatment at her hands, 'twas a miracle. Perhaps he'd have fared better with the men who attacked him than he had with her, she thought with disgust.

What had possessed her? She was generally even-tempered and patient, able to weigh all sides of a situation, to listen and hold her temper in rein no matter the provocation. Yet her behavior toward this fascinating stranger was as foreign to her as he was, as though a different person altogether had suddenly inhabited her traitorous body. Her thoughts and actions felt so new, so odd, that she scarce recognized herself.

Enough of this maundering self-pity, she cautioned herself as she sat back on her heels and considered his still features in the flickering light. Easing her hand beneath his head, she sank her fingers into his thick, soft hair, satisfied when she felt no new bumps on his poor battered skull.

She checked his wounds to make certain they'd not begun to bleed again, eased him down onto his pallet, and adjusted his bandages before settling the damp compress on his brow. She drew a soft wool blanket over him and smoothed it into place with a sigh. There was naught more she could do for him now, save watch over him as he slept.

Julianna slid around and leaned her shoulder against the wall, keeping her gaze fixed on the bruise-marred symmetry of his face. Memories of the feel of his whiskers beneath her fingers, of his surprisingly soft lips brushing her own, would guarantee she'd get no rest herself this night.

'Twas just as well, for considering the blows

to his head—several of which she'd caused by her own carelessness—she'd best keep watch over him to ensure he'd suffered no additional harm. She might as well enjoy the wakeful hours by reliving the brief contact they'd shared, for she doubted 'twould be an experience she'd ever know again.

Will woke alone the next time. Given what he thought he remembered from before—if it wasn't a dream—he wasn't sure whether that fact pleased him or not. He'd be happy to welcome the sweet-smelling siren he'd cradled upon his aching body once again, though he could certainly live without another battering by the anger-filled harpy she'd become.

He opened one eyelid with care, grateful he'd been cautious when the faint light seeping through the open shutters filled his head with a searing pain. Squeezing his eyes closed, he let his other senses explore the chamber, seeking a sound, a scent, the feel of another person nearby.

Seeking *her*.

He quieted his breathing and waited. He could sense no one else. Best to use the time to inventory his aches and injuries while he had the chance.

He felt battered enough to hurt even while at rest, of a certainty, but not so incapacitated as to keep him from fighting should he need to. His head felt nigh ready to fall off, but he'd suffered that same sensation once or twice after a night of hard drinking in Ireland and survived it. He couldn't blame a cask of usquebaugh this time, however.

Blame his own idiocy, more like, or his lack of attention. To be attacked from above like the veriest untried lad… He'd been taught better—aye, and his instincts alone should have warned him even though his attention had wandered.

Had he grown so complaisant since he'd been knighted that he'd become mindless and soft? If so, he deserved whatever he got. At least he'd survived—and no one at l'Eau Clair would know of his stupidity.

Assuming he ever returned home. For all he knew, he was a prisoner here, held by the same knaves who set upon him. Perhaps the woman had been but another of their weapons, more subtle, meant to torture him into madness with her body.

Or with her temper.

He shook his head in disgust at his mawkish thoughts, an act he regretted at once. By God, but his skull throbbed! He'd fought near as wounded as this before, though he'd rather not do so again if he could avoid it. But until he knew where he was and who held him, he'd be wise to remain alert and ready to take advantage of any opportunity.

He dared not allow his vigilance to lapse again.

Nor would he let himself fall victim to the woman once more, should she return. Neither female wiles nor warrior ways would tempt him, he vowed, no matter how appealing she appeared in either guise.

The door hinges squeaked and the door swung wide, sending a draught of cool air into the room. The scent of spice and flowers flowed over him, as noticeable this time as before. His sweet-smelling temptress had returned.

Will fought back a smile and composed himself to remain still and silent while she entered the room and shut the door.

She crossed the chamber, her boot heels tapping lightly on the plank floor, and dropped to her knees beside his pallet. Her hand rested cool and light upon his brow for but a moment before she rose and moved several paces away.

Will waited as long as his patience could bear

to ease his eyes open. Better prepared for the sensation of light on his aching eyes, he forced himself to turn his head to his left, where he'd heard her go.

Pain forgotten, he surged to his knees at the sight that met his gaze.

The woman stood nearby, the message pack he'd worn slung over his shoulder open in one hand, the bundle of Lord Rannulf's messages from within the leather bag clutched under her arm. Even as he struggled to his feet, she muttered a curse and carelessly stuffed the letters back into the pack.

Except for one. Before he could stop her, she'd cracked the wax seal on the parchment square and shook it open. The color fled her face and her words grew louder and more foul.

By the rood, what if she'd opened the message from Rannulf to Pembroke and the king? Though he was unaware of the contents, of a surety 'twas nothing for her eyes.

Will gathered himself and lunged toward her. They fell back against the wall, the bag at their feet. "What do you think you're doing? Put that down, you meddlesome wench—now!" he cried as he reached for the parchment she still held clutched tight in her hand. "Have you no respect for another's privacy?" She jerked away and he caught her by the arm.

She fought against his hold, a fury cloaked in long brown hair and an anger he could feel in her shaking body. "Meddlesome, am I?" she snarled back he pressed her against the wall. "Traitor!"

The letter caught between them, they stared at each other.

Breath held tight in his chest, Will waited.

Chapter Four

Birkland Manor, Nottinghamshire

Sir Richard Belleville ignored the usual filth and noisy disorder that engulfed the bailey and made his way to the stable by a roundabout route guaranteed to afford him privacy. His irritation rose; the fact that he must skulk like a thief from one place to another in what was essentially his own keep grated mightily on his already-short temper.

Damn Rannulf FitzClifford anyway! Birkland was but a small part of the territory FitzClifford held for both himself and his wife. 'Twas a wonder he should recall 'twas his to command. But remember it he did, far too often for Richard's peace of mind. The steadfast nobleman and his well-connected friends made Richard's life a constant battle, as he sought to balance the commands and desires of Birkland's owner against his own more profitable aspirations.

How could a man of wealth and power such as Lord Rannulf maintain his allegiance to a boy king, rather than take full advantage of the opportunity provided to put a true leader—one who would reward his friends well—in his place? The fact that Lord William Marshal, the vaunted Earl of Pembroke, stood as regent and advisor to young King Henry made little difference, so far as Richard could see. Pah, the man was ancient, a long way past his prime.

What did it matter that he'd been the most notable warrior in all England once, when that time had been decades ago? He was so old, 'twould be a miracle if he recognized his own vassals now. 'Twas a mystery why anyone would swear fealty to such a man and remain loyal to him and their weak king—and a misery for Richard, since his own loyalty rested wherever he could find the best prospect for personal gain.

And now to have one of FitzClifford's lackeys nosing about... Generally Lord Rannulf sent orders by way of a messenger, not a trusted knight from his personal troop. Sir William Bowman had been a part of Lord Rannulf's inner circle since before he'd won his spurs.

Something must have made FitzClifford suspicious about where Richard's allegiance lay. What other reason could Bowman have had to break his journey at Birkland? To deliver a message from Lord Rannulf that said next to nothing, while affording Bowman the opportunity to pry into Richard's affairs? It seemed impossible that word of his activities could have reached FitzClifford, who dwelt in one of the most remote parts of the kingdom—and so swiftly, too—but he could think of no other reason for Bowman's visit.

If the truth of Richard's involvement in the plans to overthrow the young king came to light, the best he could hope for would be a swift death. No matter that he saw no sin in working to aid those with some power to gain it all; others would see his actions as treason.

He'd simply have to make certain he remained on the side that won.

He strode into the shadowy depths of the stable, shuddering at the sudden chill that skittered down his spine. The darkness brought to mind the torture, maiming and worse that had haunted his dreams in the two nights since Bowman had arrived at Birkland. A traitor's reward—or the fears of a guilty man, mayhap—but also a powerful spur to goad him toward the successful completion of his plans.

Escorting Bowman on his way—into the maze-like depths of Sherwood, Richard reflected, giving a satisfied chuckle—had been a masterstroke. The man had even thanked him for his consideration! If the man found his way out of the wood, 'twould certainly delay his journey.

If he survived…

Yet Richard couldn't quite rid himself of the sensation that he had an arrow aimed at his back as he stood on the battlements, poised and ready to help him lose his balance and propel to his doom.

Although he'd sent two of his own trusted men after Bowman later, to do whatever necessary to ensure that the man never left the infamous forest, his uneasiness had yet to diminish.

Perhaps the fact that he had heard nothing from the pair of worthless idiots since they'd gone out after Bowman accounted for his continuing apprehension.

He'd taken care of every detail, he was sure of it. He couldn't hide the fact that Bowman had entered Birkland—unfortunately too many people had seen and spoken with him for that—but Richard stood ready, if necessary, to swear Bowman hadn't delivered any messages from Lord Rannulf to him.

In the event Bowman's effects should survive though he did not, the message from Lord Rannulf, slipped back into the pack while Bowman slept, had been resealed with wax so neatly, anyone examining the contents of Bowman's pack would never realize it had already been opened.

If anyone should come looking for Bowman, Richard would claim he'd never read Fitz-Clifford's missive before Bowman left Birkland. It should work; his ability to feign innocence had served him well all his life. He'd no reason to believe the skill would abandon him now.

After all, 'twas possible Bowman had forgotten to deliver the letter, was it not?

'Twas a shame he hadn't dared to relieve Bowman of the other messages he'd carried. He'd like to have gotten his hands on them, since Bowman had been on his way to Pembroke's camp at Lincoln. There was no telling what important missive he might have brought; perhaps something useful to Richard's plans, or his associates' goals. What a feat 'twould be if he could gain possession of important information to pass along to the leaders of their rebellion!

If his men had not only stopped Bowman, but brought back his pack... Hell, he cared little if they didn't stop Bowman, if only they'd stolen the letters.

Straw rustled deep in the far corner of the large building, distracting Richard from his musings. "There ye are, milord." Johan spoke from the gloom. "I been waitin' for ye a long time. Beginnin' to think ye mightn't o'got my message."

His eyes still adjusting to the dim light, Richard crossed to where the leader of his small, private troop of mercenaries leaned against the door of a narrow stall tucked behind the hay crib. As always, insolence lent the man's pox-scarred face a leering appearance that made Richard wonder how far Johan could be trusted.

Thus far he'd obeyed Richard's directives. He'd proven he could be relied upon—indeed, that he was highly skilled—in carrying out any task, including murder, abduction and questioning obstinate prisoners. So long as his price was met. Richard had had no cause for complaint.

Thus far.

"Your message said you'd something important to show me, something to do with Bowman," he said, low-voiced. "I didn't intend to await you in the bailey to see it, along with everyone else out there." He peered into the stall, then spun round to Johan and, using both hands, hauled him up by the front of his tunic and shook him. "You lack-wit," he ground out. "You called me to the stable to see a *horse?*"

Johan's feet skimmed the dirt floor; he grabbed hold of Richard's hands, wrenched them from his tunic and thrust them away from him. He stumbled, caught his balance and lunged back into Richard's face. "Ye better watch yerself, milord," he snarled. "Don't want to push me too far. Could be my price'll go up, to account for yer ill manners. Or mayhap I'll find me another master, one who'll treat me better." He jerked his tunic and belt into position, his right hand lingering on the long dirk sheathed at his waist. "Then where'd ye be, eh, milord Richard?" Johan's ugly face twisted into a sneer. "You'd not find another could take the place o' me so easy."

His foul breath gusted over Richard's face, nigh strong enough to overpower the usual stable stench. Muttering a curse at the unfortunate truth of Johan's threat, Richard turned away and stared into the stall again.

"Tell me about this horse," Richard demanded. He unlatched the door and entered the stall to take a closer look at the sturdy black gelding. "'Tis a fine enough animal, but I see nothing remarkable about it."

Johan leaned against the doorframe and nodded. "Aye. It ain't nothin' special, 'cept when ye know who it belongs to." He grinned. "Or belonged to, mayhap. This be Sir William's mount, milord, what he rode into the wood. We found no sign o' Bowman, but his horse, still wearin' his saddle and all his gear, we found wanderin' out near the border wi' the Tower."

"Christ's bones!" Richard slammed his hand against the wall. The pain provided an adequate substitute for the urge to roar his frustration. "What about the men I sent after Bowman? Why didn't they have the beast? And Bowman's body, for that matter." He took a calming breath. "I don't imagine you found any signs of a struggle, something to show *they* found him, at least?"

"No one's seen 'em since they set out after him yesterday afternoon." Johan shrugged. "Could Bowman have killed 'em, d'ye think?" he added, his repulsive features slanting into a curious smile. "If he had, we'd ha' found 'em out there, most like. I'd wonder if they took their pay and run off, 'cept they only got a part o' it." He slipped his knife free, used the point to pick at his teeth and spat. "Besides, they know what I'd do to 'em if I caught 'em at that." He sheathed the dirk. "It's bad for business."

Calmer now, Richard reached out and stroked the gelding. The beast shied away, nearly crushing Johan against the doorframe before he could leap aside. "Nasty bastard, he is," Johan muttered from a safe distance away. "He gave us nothin' but trouble most o' the way back here. Miserable bastard! Never did care much for horses." He turned and dug through the hay piled near the stall and dragged out a saddle and several packs. "Here's all we found," he said.

Ignoring the saddle, Richard grabbed the packs and began to paw through them. Naught but clothing and some supplies... Not a sign of what he sought, however. Disgusted, he shoved the packs aside. "Was there a small leather pouch tied to the saddle? About so big—'' he gestured with his hands ''—with a strap long enough to sling it over your shoulder.''

Johan shook his head. ''This is everythin'. Maybe Bowman was wearin' it, or dropped it someplace.''

''Then we need Bowman. Send someone out into the forest again, and tell them to look more carefully this time! Sherwood's got hiding places aplenty—far too many for there to have been a thorough search so soon.'' He knelt beside the packs and rummaged through the contents once more. Nothing! He stuffed everything back inside them and held them out to Johan. ''Take these with you—the horse, too. I don't want anyone asking questions about Bowman. 'Tis best if it looks as if he disappeared far from here, so no one suspects we had anything to do with it.''

Richard stood. ''Keep looking.'' Turning, he began to walk away, then paused and looked back, giving the mercenary his most menacing glare. ''The next time I see you, you'd better have something valuable for me.''

Chapter Five

Julianna kept tight hold of the missive she'd found in her patient's pack, despite his unyielding grip on her fingers and the way his body pinned hers to the rough plaster wall. He might be bigger and stronger than she, but from the way he trembled and rested his weight against her—as much for support, she'd guess, as to hold her in place—she'd only to remain patient and wait a bit before she won this battle.

Before she could read the rest of the letter addressed to her enemy.

His warmth sank through her clothing and into her flesh, tempting her traitorous body anew and reminding her what a fool she'd been. To trust a stranger for even a moment, to lust for a stranger's touch, when she knew naught of whether he be ally or foe.

Dear God, she must be mad!

The sense of betrayal gave her the determination to slip from beneath his weight. He tightened his grasp, however, his hand fisted around hers, the parchment crumpling within her hold as he spun her around to face him.

"Have a care who you call traitor, milady," he warned, bending so close to her, his whiskers scraped along her jaw. "Else I'll be forced to judge *you* traitor instead." A swift glance at his face showed no weakness now, only a steady resolve she'd do well to heed. Though his blue eyes burned with fever and pain, she couldn't mistake the outrage lurking there. Had she insulted him? Could it be that he was no more a traitor than she?

Or mayhap he was simply better at disguising his true nature.

She pushed away from him, making him reel for a moment before he caught his balance against the wall. He retained his grip on her hand, however, maddening her all the more. "With what reason?" she asked. "I am a true and loyal subject of our king—"

"Are you?" he ground out, straightening to his full height and taking a step toward her. "I know nothing of you, lady—not so much as who you are, or the name of this place."

"Tuck's Tower," she told him with hard-won calm. "Do you know of it?"

He shook his head. Then, his lips twisting into a mocking smile at odds with the steel in his gaze, he tugged her nearer. "But who are you? A lady dressed in warrior's garb... I've only known of one other woman who would do so. 'Tis uncommon, you must admit—rare enough to raise questions in a curious man's mind. Do you command the defense of Tuck's Tower, milady?" With his free hand he cupped her chin, then slid his fingers down along her neck and over her shoulder before stopping, his open palm pressed lightly just above her breast. "'Tis a puzzle certain to entice a man," he murmured. "Or could it be you're simply a siren, meant to lure a man to your bed and render him your slave?"

The low timbre of his voice sent a shiver of awareness down her spine and made her heartbeat thrum faster beneath his hand—he found her alluring?—before the insult of his words and bold caress made its way to her poor besotted brain. He mocked her, more likely.

Though it took all her resolve, she reached up and yanked his hand away. "Hardly a siren," she scoffed with a mirthless laugh. "Nor a puzzle, either. I am simply a woman, though one with no wiles to tempt a man. I scarce appear a woman at all." She grabbed the loose-fitting tail of her shirt and held it out. "A man's garb, stout armor and a strong sword are hardly the weapons of enticement, though they serve me well enough."

"Aye, they suit you well indeed, milady," he said, his gaze roaming along her from head to toe, lingering upon her legs in their snug braes before rising to her face and pinning her fast within the heated blue of his eyes. Sudden awareness hardened his features; he shook his head and glanced away for a moment. When he turned back to her, his expression pensive, he added, "Mayhap you're naught but an outlaw or a robber, then, setting upon any hapless traveler who passes your way. This is Sherwood Forest, after all."

How dare he accuse her? "The blow to your head has clearly scrambled your brain. I saved your worthless life, you idiot! Is that the act of a robber?" she demanded.

Throughout their discourse he'd retained his hold on her hand and the parchment she'd found in his pack—a fact she had scarce noted till now, to her shame—but her fury made her aware of it, and gave her the impetus to jerk herself free.

It infuriated her all the more that he let her.

"You'll find no outlaws here—" She clamped her mouth shut, afraid her temper might lead her into dangerous waters. She drew in a calming breath. "Nor traitors, either."

Julianna wanted nothing more than to pound out her anger and frustration upon his chest, but she greatly feared that to touch him thus would do naught but beguile her to lay her hands on him in other, less aggressive ways.

Sweet Mary save her, had she lost all sense of self-preservation, of right and wrong? The man called her robber and traitor, and what did she do but seek to draw his attention to her in any way she could. She knew better.

She stepped away before her temper led her into worse foolishness, pausing an arm's length away. 'Twould be better to ease the tension between them than to aggravate it further. Closing her eyes, she combed her hair back from her face with one hand and eased her grip on the parchment with the other. "Thus far we've managed to do nothing but provoke each other," she said, trying to infuse her voice with a note of apology. "Surely we can be more civil than that—and resolve our differences, whatever they might be."

"I'm willing if you are," he said, his expression amused.

Did he doubt she was capable of civility? If so, he'd reason, she had to admit. She'd shown scant evidence of courtesy to him.

Though she did know the trappings of well-mannered behavior, she'd look a complete fool to curtsey in shirt and braes. He'd have to be satisfied with polite words, not actions.

She eased her crushing grip on the letter and lowered her hands to her sides. "I am Julianna d'Arcy," she said, nodding. "I bid you welcome to Tuck's Tower."

"You are lady of this keep?"

A strange question, but asked in a most reasonable tone—mildly curious, not accusing or judgmental in any way. "Aye, and defender of it, as well."

He nodded, then, taking her free hand in his, he swept a low bow. "Lady Julianna, I am William Bowman, a simple knight in the service of

Lord Rannulf FitzClifford.'' His gaze fixed upon hers, he raised her hand to his lips. '''Tis a pleasure to meet you,'' he said, the words causing nigh as much effect as the feel of his fingers stroking her palm and his mouth upon her flesh.

Julianna nearly snatched her hand away before he straightened and released her, so intense was her reaction to the change in his voice. 'Twas all she could do to suppress the quiver skimming over her skin at the sound of it, to resist the urge to lean closer to him, to bask in the feel of that audible touch.

Oh, but he was a clever man! No doubt he used that low, caressing murmur as a weapon to manipulate women; he'd be a fool not to.

But he'd soon discover it had no effect upon her.

She'd see to that, she vowed, no matter how difficult it was to accomplish.

No matter how much it went counter to the inclination of her suddenly traitorous body.

She drew herself up to her full height, tried for an imperious bearing, met his gaze and gave a cool nod. ''Now then, Sir William—''

''Will,'' he said with an easy smile.

Did he think to cozen her with but a smile?

She'd dealt with charming men before—aye, she knew any number of persuasive scoundrels. She also knew 'twas best to give them no chance to attempt to work their wiles upon her. It did naught but annoy her, though with Sir William, she feared her reaction would be anything but annoyance.

He'd not find her an easy target.

"Sir William, what were you doing wandering through Sherwood alone?" she asked.

Will held Lady Julianna's gaze, silently pondering the sudden change in her bearing. Thus far in their brief acquaintance he'd seen her soft and yielding beneath him, and fierce as any warrior. But this serene woman, wearing the mantle of command so effortlessly on her shoulders, showed him another facet of her altogether—for despite the well-worn men's garb she wore, he could never mistake her for anything but a noble lady.

He weighed the determination in her amber eyes, his mind—still awhirl from the battering he'd taken—pondering the best way to proceed. She still held one of Lord Rannulf's letters clutched in her hand, and the leather pouch he'd carried them in lay on the floor behind her.

Though 'twould be a pleasure indeed to take his time with her, he'd no business toying with a lady.

Nor did he have time to dally here; Lord Rannulf had set him a task, one he'd yet to complete. It was too important for him to let anything go awry.

Could he bargain with her for the letter? Or would she simply hand it over to him if he asked?

Her lips firmed; her expression, though weary, showed not a whit of compliance. Though she'd been civil, indeed, 'twas clear she'd not simply give in. His pulse quickened in anticipation.

He smiled, and Lady Julianna's chin rose, her look of stubbornness growing more pronounced. Though he knew he'd have to work to regain his possessions, there was no reason he couldn't enjoy the process. He'd always enjoyed a good fight, especially a verbal one.

And it appeared his warrior lady had every intention of enjoining him in battle.

Chapter Six

Will folded his arms and leaned his shoulders back against the wall, more to provoke Lady Julianna, truth be told, than because he needed the wall for support. "If I asked you most politely for my pack and the letters, would you give them to me and allow me to continue on my way?"

"You're in no condition to go anywhere at the moment, save back to your pallet," she said, her tart tone a perfect accompaniment to the fire in her eyes and the faint tinge of color mounting her cheeks. "So I see no reason to return any of your belongings to you just yet." She stooped to pick up the leather pouch from the floor, her dark hair swinging like a cloak about her and shielding him from her view.

Will took advantage of the moment to reach for

the dagger he kept tucked in the top of his boot, only to realize that his feet were bare—though even if they'd left his boots on, they weren't likely to have left a weapon so easily at hand.

Not that he'd have used it against her, in any case. But as a threat, if necessary...

Lady Julianna rose, shook her hair out of the way and faced him before he could disguise the movement as anything but what it had been. She tucked the parchment into the bag, closed the flap and swung the strap over her shoulder, giving the pouch a final pat that made the bundle of messages crackle.

Reaching down to her own boot, she slipped a dagger free. "Were you looking for this?" she asked. She straightened, tossing the dagger and catching it by the hilt with the ease of long practice. "It seems a fine piece," she mused as she inspected the design etched into the blade. "Well-balanced, and well-used, too, from the look of it."

"'Twas habit, nothing more." Will shrugged and leaned back against the rough plaster as though he hadn't a care in the world. He needed the wall's support now, but Lady Julianna didn't need to know his head had begun to spin so badly he could scarcely stand.

She glanced up at him from beneath her lashes. "Did you really expect I would permit a stranger, even an injured stranger, to remain armed within my walls?" Her amber gaze never leaving his, she bent and returned the knife to her boot.

He shook his head, regretting it at once; not only did it hurt like the devil, but his vision began to blur around the edges. "'Twould have made no difference either way. I doubt I'd manage to leave here alone, with naught but a blade to protect me."

Lady Julianna's expression went from stern to alarmed in an instant. What had caused the sudden change? he wondered as he pushed away from the wall and spun toward the door.

His legs folded beneath him; he saw nothing save a blur of brown and white moving his way as he crumpled to the floor.

Julianna rushed toward Will as soon as she saw his face go white and his body begin to list to the side, but she couldn't reach him in time to prevent him from dropping to the hard oak planks at her feet. "Sweet Mary save you, you fool!" Sinking to her knees beside him, she gathered him into her arms. "This is becoming a habit I'd rather not repeat."

His head lolled against her chest, his mouth much too near her unbound breasts. Sudden suspicion made her shift him away from her none too gently, giving him a poke in the ribs, and scramble back from him.

What if this was but a ploy to play upon her sympathy, to disarm her and take the letters? He could tie her up and slip from the room without being seen—could escape the keep with no one the wiser till they wondered where she was and came looking for her!

What a fool *she* had been!

She ripped the leather message pouch from her shoulder and tossed it across the chamber, noting when she did so that her palms felt wet. The sharp smell of blood reached her even as she raised her hands and saw the crimson streaks covering her fingers.

He couldn't feign that!

He hadn't so much as moaned when she'd poked him and let him collapse to the floor, either.

Remorse filled her, lending haste to her movements. She returned to his side and checked his bandages. Blood seeped from both the one on his neck and his arm, and must have been doing so for some time. When she slid her hand under him to shift him from the floor to the pallet, she could tell the back of his shirt was soaked with it as well.

She situated him on the low bed and eased the garment over his head. It looked as bad as it had felt—soggy with the blood that now besmirched them both. There was so much of it; how could *he* not have noticed? 'Twas no wonder he'd collapsed—she was surprised it hadn't happened sooner. She turned him onto his side; a rivulet of red trailed down his back, and a smaller one trickled down his front, pooling in the thick mass of dark blond curls covering his chest and stomach.

So much blood...but bright and newly spilled, from the look of it.

Perhaps when he'd fallen earlier the wounds had opened. And when she'd lain beneath him, he'd propped himself up on his arms, she recalled—that might have added to the problem.

It might explain why he hadn't been aware of it *then,* if he'd been as distracted as she had been, but afterward....

Afterward they'd argued.

Julianna unwound the linen strip from around Will's arm and frowned at the ugly sight. 'Twas swollen and red, oozing blood and worse. She hadn't stitched the cut, hoping it would mend fine on its own—and if he'd put no pressure on it, mayhap it would have.

Or perhaps not. In truth, she hated to sew, especially if she was sticking her needle into someone's skin. She did a bad enough job when using a piece of cloth, but to mangle a man's flesh in that manner was far worse.

If only Mary hadn't been so far gone in drink that she couldn't help.

If only *she* hadn't been such a coward.

Sighing, she gently pressed the cloth over the arm wound and peeked under the edge of the bandage about his neck. From the look of it, stitches would improve that situation as well.

Now Will would pay the price of her cowardice, for the cuts appeared puffy and felt hot to the touch—'twould be far more painful for him than if she'd done the deed the night before.

She wiped the blood from her fingers and laid one hand on his chest above his heart. Heat radiated from him, though his heart pulsed steady and strong beneath her touch. A fever, too—not unusual in these circumstances, but one more problem to deal with before she could pronounce him healed and decided what to do with him.

Keep him captive?

Send him on his way?

If she could.

'Twould be foolish to try to make sense of what that means, Julianna! she cautioned herself. Shaking her head as though 'twould clear her mind, she returned her attention to Will.

Julianna gave but brief thought to calling for Mary's help; no doubt the woman still lay on the floor of the barracks. 'Twould not be the first time she'd been useless for several days after going on a drunken binge, nor was it like to be the last.

Lowering her head, she sought for patience out of the frustration that rose within her at the thought. She would have sent Mary on her way long since, if only she hadn't sworn to her parents that she'd care for everyone who dwelled within her domain.

Perhaps things would be different—of a certainty, her life would be—if she'd been in truth the noble lady those outside Tuck's Tower believed her to be—

The Bride of the Tower.

She gave a mirthless laugh as she called the foolish legend to mind. It said she was fated to wed a man worthy of Lady Marian's daughter, to provide for their people and care for them as Julianna's father—her true father—would have, had he lived.

But the only groom she could foresee in her future was Tuck's Tower itself. She felt wedded to the place most truly, and could not imagine finding any man who would permit her to be herself, to continue to serve her people in every way she could. What potential suitors she'd had—and there'd not been many she'd met face-to-face—had tended to run fast and far when they'd learned Lady Julianna could wield a sword most competently, shoot a bow with her father's legendary skill, but knew little and cared less about embroidering, spinning or managing a household.

Most likely the sight of her, armed and armor-clad, unabashedly a warrior, had quelled their passion a mite as well.

To blazes with the lot of them! She could manage on her own.

And she had to admit, Tuck's Tower made as fine a husband as any. She could dress as she pleased, and she need not worry about arguments, orders or demands for her to abandon her unlady-like ways.

That thought raised her spirits.

They crashed down to earth again when she gazed at the man sprawled before her. A castle made a cold bedmate on the long, lonely nights, nor was it apt to fire her blood and flesh the way her brief contact with Sir William Bowman had done.

Yet for all she knew, he'd a woman or a wife— or both, mayhap—back home among his people, wherever that was. Womanly women, ladies who knew how to dress, to sing, to do all the ladylike activities that had held not the faintest trace of interest for her.

Until now.

Would Will find her attractive if she dragged out the coffer of clothes her mother had sewn for her years ago, before it became obvious Julianna would not wear them? If she draped her body in silks and fine woolens, laced tight about her ribs till she thought she'd not be able to breathe? Tamed the unruly mass of her hair, draped a gauzy veil over it, and learned to move with an angel's grace? What if she sat silently beside him at table, head bowed demurely, awaiting his pleasure?

Even if he did find that woman to his taste, would Julianna consider him—or a man like him, one who made her yearn to be a woman in every way with him, *for* him—worth the sacrifices she would have to make?

Will groaned and shifted on the pallet, nudging her from her reverie and returning her attention to more important matters.

Just look at how he'd jumbled her wits, made her forget too many important things—and she knew so little of him, save that he was handsome, could be charming, appeared strong—and he made her feel in a way no man had ever done before.

'Twas not enough, however, to tempt her to change her life, to venture into an uncertain territory where she had no dominion.

Aye, she was a coward indeed.

Julianna thought again of calling for Mary—for anyone—to assist her with her unpleasant task, then shook her head at her own spinelessness. Muttering beneath her breath lest she wake Will, for she'd far rather stitch him up while he wouldn't move, protest or fight, she retrieved her basket of simples from beside the door and crossed the small chamber to throw wide the heavy shutters for more light.

Whether he would remain silent and motionless

once she began the gruesome task could help her
judge the severity of his condition.

As she held together the edges of the wound
on Will's arm and sank the needle into his flesh,
his skin barely twitched despite the pain.

She, however, felt every awkward stab as
keenly as if she were the one being stitched up—
a phantom sting, true, but no less painful than if
'twere real.

She lowered her head and rested her brow on
her arm for a moment, whispering prayers to calm
herself. More pleas to the Virgin might help them
both, for 'twas all she could do to keep her hands
steady.

Though she lacked a lady's skill at needlework,
the least she could do was attempt to mend his
poor torn flesh neatly. Besides, she'd seen more
than once the results of a wound ill-mended; thick
scars, or crookedly sewn gashes, could interfere
with the freedom of movement needed to wield a
sword or other weapons.

She could do no less than try to restore this
warrior to his former strength.

Julianna closed her eyes for a moment and pic-
tured Will uninjured, free to swing a sword or
brandish a knife. 'Twas an image to light her spir-

its! God willing, in time he would be able to do so again.

The thought settled her nerves—though it also made her heart race a bit, she had to admit. *Enough, Julianna! Calm yourself, you fool.* She shook her head and drew the mantle of warrior about herself. 'Twas another battle to be fought and won, nothing more.

Nerves settled, she applied herself to the task, slow and steady, allowing her thoughts to drift back to their previous path.

To the man before her, and what changes she'd brought upon herself and her people by carrying him through the gates of Tuck's Tower. No matter the outcome of his time here, or the truth of his purpose in the area, she could already sense the changes within herself brought about from their chance encounter.

She felt bolder, more free, yet more reserved— a wariness of revealing too much of herself, even as she wanted to learn everything she could about him. Nay, not only about Will, but also about the world she'd seldom considered—the world that existed beyond her tiny corner of it.

He made her want to expand her horizons, to

experience life in ways she'd never before envisioned.

Seldom had she been overly cautious. Even in those situations where she had hesitated to proceed, more often than not she'd managed to gather up her nerve and venture onward.

Could she do so with this man?

And if she did, would he be worth the risk?

Chapter Seven

Julianna poured the last of the water from the pitcher into the basin, savoring the cool bite of it as she dipped her hands in, then scooped it up to rinse her face. Despite the chill, it did little to wash away the weariness dogging her every move, but at least she felt a bit cleaner and more refreshed.

She'd scarcely left the small room next to hers the last two days, for Will's fever had become worse after he'd collapsed and she'd sewn him up. Only now that he appeared on the mend—his fever had lessened, and his wounds were beginning to heal properly—did she feel free to quit his chamber and tend to herself and some of the business left undone while he'd been so ill.

Though he'd slept almost constantly through

the past two days, it had been clear to her that when he spoke—during the brief times when his eyes had been open—that he'd no idea where he was or what was real. She doubted he'd even noticed her. He'd clearly been out of his senses the entire time.

She didn't know who he had thought he'd been speaking to, but it must have been someone he knew well and felt comfortable with, for he'd smiled and chuckled often—the low, deep sound raking over her like a touch—and his tone and words had been straightforward and easy…almost intimate.

She refused to consider what that meant. It had sounded as though he spoke with a woman, though not a lover or wife. Still, what would she know of such things? A sister, perhaps? It mattered not who it was, at any rate. His personal life was none of her business. She'd do well to remind herself of that fact, and concentrate upon making him well so he could return to his life and whoever he'd left behind.

Still, as she kept watch by his side, she couldn't help but notice what he said. He'd enlivened her vigil and kept her awake when all she'd wanted was to curl up on the floor beside his pallet and give in to her weariness. When he'd sounded somewhat clear-minded, he'd captured her curiosity and kept her wits well employed as she sought details of his life from his words. 'Twas a blessing he'd kept her so well entertained, she thought wryly, for she didn't want to miss what he said.

He certainly had a good imagination. When his discourse had rambled from conversation to delirium, it had provided a welcome distraction from her concern as his fever rose and his injuries festered.

Bits and pieces about dragons and virtuous maids, crazed Irish warriors and a dog large enough for a child to ride upon…each tale sounded more fantastical than the next. If not for the fact of Will's obvious suffering, she'd have enjoyed trying to cobble together what he was trying to say into some sort of tale. He clearly had a knack for storytelling, and was evidently a bit of a prankster, as well, if she judged by some of the things he'd related.

She'd not taken nearly as much pleasure in his words once his imagination had turned to stories of the infamous outlaws of Sherwood Forest. At first she'd been surprised he knew of them.

Though he spoke French the same as she, she could hear a difference in his accent; he was from some other part of England altogether, she'd guess. How, then, had he heard about Tuck, Little John, Will Scarlet and others? She'd no notion the tales—or legends, for the stories had swelled to mythical proportions—had become so widely renowned.

As for the hero and heroine of the legends— 'twas clear he'd idolized both Maid Marian FitzWalter and Robin of the Hood. When he'd been a child, perhaps? At times it had sounded as though he'd been playing at outlaws with other children, most often one named Gilles.

Mind still awhirl with questions—but more revived now—she dried her face and hands on a piece of linen, then filled the basin with warm water from the bucket on the hearth. Stripping off her wrinkled clothes, she washed, emptying her mind of thought as she took pleasure in the simple act.

Finally dressed in a fresh shirt and braes, she sat in the sun by the window. She could pretend for a while that she'd nothing more important to do than daydream, to brush her hair and allow her thoughts to roam wherever they chose. The rhythmic motion of the brush might soothe her, untie the knot of tension holding her neck and shoulders within its grip.

Unfinished business, in the form of maidservants asking questions and soldiers needing direction, would interrupt her soon enough. Meanwhile, the light and warmth lured her to savor a quiet moment for herself. She sprawled on the window seat like a cat in a sunbeam and relished the brief respite.

Taking her time, she drew her brush through the mass of her hair, unknotting the tangled strands and allowing her thoughts—as they seemed wont to do—to shift back to Will yet again.

What would he think if he were to discover that Marian FitzWalter and Robin of the Hood were not merely legends, but had been real people?

Her parents.

Would he even believe it?

It was not widely known beyond Sherwood, but 'twas no secret, either. However, he'd no reason to suspect such a startling truth. She bore the name of Lord Roger d'Arcy, the man who'd wed her mother, who had been a father to her in every way save by blood. She'd loved him and respected him, given thanks often that her lady mother had seen fit to accept his offer of his name, his home and heart.

He'd been a dear man. He'd loved her without reservation and taught her everything she'd asked, in spite of the fact that she'd demanded to be shown a son's duties, not a daughter's. Perhaps her reason for refusing the suitors who'd wanted to wed the Bride of the Tower had been because she knew she could never find another man so sensible as her father.

What would her life have been like, Julianna wondered as she had so often before, had her mother remained in the forest with her outlaw lover, or hidden herself away in a convent to bear her illegitimate child? Would mother and child have been dead after a hard winter spent in Sherwood, or would they have remained shut away behind cloistered walls in a lifetime of shame and penitence for her parents' sins?

If her mother had loved Robin more deeply than she'd cared for the man she'd married, it had never been apparent to her daughter, at least. Lady Marian had seldom mentioned her time with Robin, leaving Julianna with the sense that 'twas too painful for her to recall. 'Twas beyond her ken to imagine her gentle mother roaming Sherwood with a band of outlaws and a roguish priest, and she'd never understood what could have prompted her to do so.

Within Julianna's memory, Lady Marian had never sought adventure; 'twas difficult to imagine. She had been a true lady, a devoted and loyal wife to Lord Roger d'Arcy, and the home they'd created for Julianna had nestled her in a sanctuary of care and security.

Until recent years had brought an end to it.

The political situation in Nottingham had quieted after the tumultuous time when Robin and his men had been a force in the area. The d'Arcys had kept a distance from their neighbors for many years, occasionally receiving news of the outside world from Lord Phillip d'Arcy, Lord Roger's elder brother and overlord. Eventually, however, the unrest at the end of King John's reign had made it impossible for them to disregard what went on outside Tuck's Tower.

Once the king had died and his young son taken his place, their peace had been forever shattered.

Julianna gazed unseeing into the distance, the rich green of hills and trees a verdant blur as she stared inward at the landscape of her mind. Some neighbors she wished she'd never met, chief among them Sir Richard Belleville. The man seemed petty and power-mad, and he'd not a thought in his head beyond improving his own lot in any way he could. She could not fault him for that, up to a point, but there seemed no limits to what he'd do in order to achieve his goals.

His successes had been minor ones, though more than she'd have expected of a man who as far as she knew, had little influence beyond Birkland, and no property to call his own. Though he liked to pretend he was the lord of Birkland, in truth he was nothing more than a very minor vassal who held the place for a far-away nobleman. Should he displease his distant master, his position could disappear in an instant.

The thought had occurred to Julianna on several occasions to do what she could to bring about such displeasure—and Belleville's subsequent dismissal. Yet despite her uneasiness about him, she had scant evidence of anything more serious against him than that he possessed an arrogant and obnoxious manner.

She paused in her task, resting her brush on the window ledge and staring out at the bright blue sky. A fine fool she'd look, to try to have a man discharged from his position for possessing the same characteristics as half the men she'd met!

But how could she ignore his subtle, repeated attempts to gain dominion over Tuck's Tower, a niggling voice in her head reminded her.

She had no proof 'twas his aim, however, only suspicions and random hints of information that made no sense to her. For all she knew, his unknown master could have ordered him to expand Birkland's demesne in any way he could. 'Twould be no different than the way many holdings increased in size, she thought wryly, especially in these unsettled times.

A knock on the door brought her reflections to an end. "Come," she called, setting aside her brush and beginning to plait her now-smooth hair. Her respite over, when she'd finished she rose and went to pull on her boots.

Dora, the elderly woman who'd been her mother's maid and now served Julianna, hurried into the room, Rolf hard on her heels. The diminutive woman, arms overflowing with a bundle of clothing, halted just inside the chamber and turned on the soldier. They collided, clothing flying up and over them both.

Rolf caught Dora about the waist and held her

steady against him before she could fall over. She began to berate him at once, her words muffled by the fabric draped over her face.

"Here now, mistress, what are you about?" he demanded. He set her on her feet, tugged the shirt off her head and bent to gather up the garments from where they'd landed on the floor.

"Can't you leave milady alone for an instant?" she replied. Once he straightened she cuffed him on the arm, to no effect, and pointed for him to place the clothes on the bed. He rolled his eyes, but obeyed her silent command. "She's barely had a moment's rest in days, not since she carried home that handsome young rascal," she added with a nod toward the next chamber. "Not that he could help getting injured, I suppose."

Julianna bit back a laugh. Dora's tone left little doubt she felt Will *could* have avoided injury if he'd really tried.

Dora scarcely paused to take a breath before turning her attention back to Rolf. "As for you— barging in here without a by-your-leave…'tis a lucky thing indeed that you didn't catch Lady Julianna bathing, you mannerless lout!"

"Perhaps he'd have considered himself luckier

if he had,'' Julianna said. She chuckled at the way
Rolf's face reddened, but he grinned as well.

"Lady Julianna!" Dora scolded, rounding on
her even as she began to tidy the mess from Julianna's bath. "What would your lady mother
have said to hear such bawdy foolery from you,
may Mary bless her soul?" She crossed herself
and went right along with her work. "Have you
no shame?"

"You should know by now that I have none,"
she pointed out dryly. "Or very little, at any
rate." She picked up her dagger and Will's and
tucked one into each boot. "'Twas naught but a
harmless jape, nothing more. I'd not have said to
come in were I actually bathing. I didn't know
who was outside the door, after all."

Dora sent her a reproving look and crossed to
the bed to fold the disheveled mound of clothing.
Julianna took this as her opportunity to avoid further lectures and motioned for Rolf to accompany
her as she returned to Will's sickroom.

She was not so fortunate as to escape so easily,
however.

"I'll go sit with him, milady." Dora abandoned
the laundry and headed for the door connecting
the two chambers. Pausing with her hand on the

latch, she added, "I know you've many other things to attend to. If yon warrior has need of you, I'll send for you at once, but I'm certain I can deal with him."

Dora was right; Will had been sound asleep when she'd last looked in on him. Lord knew, she could find plenty of other tasks to occupy her, body and mind.

Besides, perhaps if she left his side for a bit, the image of his face would fade from her memory and leave her poor obsessed mind in peace.

Or not, the little voice inside her head taunted.

Consigning her traitorous wits to the cesspit where they clearly belonged, Julianna nodded to Dora and Rolf and left in search of some task to distract her from the temptation of Sir William Bowman.

Chapter Eight

Will awoke to the sound of a woman singing, and the awareness that a long time had passed since he'd last been able to think clearly. Holding his breath, he risked stretching out on the straw pallet. He didn't hurt as much as before; while his body ached, and he noted several more painful places where he could feel the sting of healing wounds, at least his head and stomach seemed vastly better than before.

Whether that would remain the case when he ventured to stand would be the true test, but he'd wait to try that till he felt a bit livelier.

Though he'd not wait too long. He didn't know how many days had passed; he knew *where* he was, at least, and how he'd come to be there.

Tuck's Tower, near Sherwood Forest.

The keep's name and location had been the cause, no doubt, of the many strange dreams of Robin of the Hood, Maid Marian and Robin's band of outlaws that had haunted his restless sleep.

As had Lady Julianna d'Arcy.

He remembered his lovely savior—or captor, he really wasn't certain precisely which she was—as well. She had haunted his dreams, too; she'd unquestionably inspired the tempting enchantress he'd encountered in some of his other imaginings.

Dreams, and feelings, he wished he could remember more completely.

He closed his eyes and concentrated. Bits of them were etched upon his memory so deeply that he'd likely remember them until his dying day, mental sensations so vivid they might have been recollections of reality, so vibrant the passage of decades could not erase their intensity.

They'd seemed quite real at the time, but he knew they were not.

His lips twisted into a grin, making him aware that his mouth felt bone dry and tasted hideous. 'Twas a good thing he'd not really be kissing Lady Julianna—or doing any of the other delight-

ful things they'd done in his imagination. If
knowledge of his wicked desires didn't send her
reeling from shock, the stench of his breath would
have been apt to do so.

He doubted the rest of him smelled much better, either—though he could have sworn that
somewhere in his disjointed thoughts was the
memory of someone bathing him. Cool, soothing
hands—had they been hers?

Of course, if Lady Julianna ever suspected the
captivating role his fevered imagination had cast
her in, she'd likely whip his dagger from her boot
and gut him—or worse!—with his own blade.

He'd deserve it, too, for thinking of a noble
lady in such a way.

Ah, but noble ladies did feel desire…and act
upon it, as well. He'd learned that soon enough
once he'd left l'Eau Clair and come into the milieu of ladies who hadn't known him since he was
an obnoxious freeman's son playing alongside
them in the dirt. Will's first sojourn at Court with
Lord Rannulf had amazed him, opening his eyes
to the veritable feast of women willing to play
any erotic game he chose.

As well as some he hadn't, he recalled with a
shudder. He'd learned to be more discerning, after

several narrow escapes from those women who were naught but insatiable harpies looking to snare a new, naive victim for their depraved entertainment.

Now *there* was a thought to avoid! He'd no desire to taint the memory of the sweet taste of Lady Julianna's lips—a real memory, that, brief but unforgettable. Nor did he wish to travel, even in memory, down that twisted road again.

Though he'd paid her small heed, he had been hazily aware of the small woman sitting by the small window, her quavery voice providing a faint background to his thoughts. He'd no sooner realized she'd stopped singing than she popped up from her seat and bustled to his side. Her wide smile revealed a surprisingly complete set of teeth for one so old. As she reached him, her faded-blue eyes seemed to disappear into her wrinkled face as she bent and, squinting, peered down at him.

"So you've decided to rejoin the land of the living, have you?" she asked, her hands busy smoothing the tangled coverlet and adjusting it over him as she spoke. Her smile undimmed, she gave the soft wool a final pat and drew a low stool close to his pallet. "You gave my mistress a scare indeed, my young sir. 'Tis happy she'll be to see how you've recovered.''

She filled a cup from a pottery jug on a nearby table and offered it to him before she settled herself on the stool. "Here. This special draught will speed your healing.''

Will shifted onto his side and brought the drink to his mouth, only to stop short when he caught a whiff of the foul brew. The old woman shook her head and pushed the cup the rest of the way. "I know it smells as though it comes straight from the cess pit, but 'tis truly a very helpful tonic.'' Before he had a chance to oppose her, she reached over and tipped the medicine into his mouth. "There now, 'tis not so bad, is it?''

It tasted worse than it smelled! Sputtering and doing his best not to gag, Will valiantly dumped the remainder of the potion down his throat and glared at the old woman still smiling so sweetly at him.

"What *is* that?'' he gasped, scarcely loud enough to be heard. He had to swallow several times and clear his throat before he could make his voice work properly. He dropped back onto the pallet. "By the Saints, woman, are you in league with the devil? What have I done that you seek to poison me?''

"Now why would I want to do that?" she asked, her tone and expression innocent—and her eyes sharp. "Is there some reason I should?"

"Not that I'm aware of." He gave her the empty cup, which still reeked of the noxious brew. Surprisingly, in spite of its effect on his throat, it hadn't bothered his stomach.

She handed him a wet cloth for his face and a small branch of mint, the leaves of which he popped into his mouth at once. "My name is Dora, not 'woman.' You'd do well to be courteous to the person who tends you, milord." Her expression as challenging as her voice was sweet, once he'd wiped his face and hands, she took away the cloth and handed him another drink. "There's no telling what sort of treatment you might receive otherwise."

"I beg your forgiveness, Dora." Feeling more refreshed, he eased himself up and gingerly propped his back against the wall. "I'm not usually so bad-mannered. 'Twas the shock. I've tasted some truly appalling brews in my life, but nothing to touch that—" *hog swill? devil's piss?* "—that healing potion." Raising an eyebrow in question, he accepted the goblet she held out, but made no attempt to bring it to his lips. "Dare I?" he asked. Despite the fresh taste of mint in his mouth, his throat clenched in anticipation of another assault.

Appearing to accept his apology, Dora smiled. "Go on, 'tis safe. It's water from our spring, nothing more. You'll not taste a fresher water anywhere, I vow," she told him. "'Tis nothing like the foul stuff you get from most castle wells."

Will took a tentative sip, then drank deeply, eager to quench his thirst and to wash the last of the rank taste from his tongue. She'd been right—twas as delicious as she'd claimed, especially brightened by the freshness of the mint.

Of course, compared to the noisome slop she'd given him earlier...

"Is there anything else I can do for you, milord? I told Lady Julianna I'd watch over you for a bit so she could get out and about." Dora refilled the goblet, not pausing for a moment in her discourse. "I had hoped she might rest, but not my lady. She's not one to lie about when there's work to be done, no matter how weary she might be. She tended you herself. She'd scarce allow anyone else to help her at all." Dora set down the pitcher and handed him the water. "Aye, she never left your side the whole time you were sick, not till your fever broke late this morn."

He drank again, more slowly now, savoring the cool liquid as it soothed his dry throat and lips.

And taking pleasure in the fact that Lady Julianna had stayed with him. "How long has it been?"

"Two days and nights you burned with fever. Your wounds began to fester, but she brought a stop to that before they got too bad!" she said with a decisive nod. "My lady shouldn't have waited so long to stitch them. If she'd but asked my counsel, I'd have told her what needed to be done—and helped her, too. Indeed, I remember the time my dear Lady Marian—"

"She sewed me up? When did she do that?" He had no recollection of it whatsoever, for which he thanked God. 'Twas a most unpleasant sensation to have a needle poked into flesh that already hurt like the devil, one he'd rather not experience again.

It seemed he'd been fortunate this time, if he could count himself fortunate to have been too out of his head to notice her stitching him up like a piece of embroidery.

"She told me you didn't realize how bad you were hurt, and that when you tried to stand the first morn you were here, you fell and broke open the wounds." Dora's expression turned questioning, her gaze sharp as she met his eyes.

Clearly the woman didn't believe that had been the truth. Did she think he'd tried to harm her mistress? He bit back a laugh. He doubted he could have hurt a defenseless babe at that point, never mind a woman as well equipped to protect herself as Lady Julianna.

He met Dora's expectant look with an innocent shrug. If Lady Julianna hadn't admitted she'd been rolling about on the floor with him—or that she'd knocked him against the wall a few times as well—'twas not for him to share that information.

"'Tis true," he assured her. "My recollection of that morning is hazy, but I know I tried to get up, and I did move around a bit."

He bit back a smile. *Aye, that he had—as had Dora's mistress.*

He hadn't noticed he was bleeding then, or that his injuries hurt any more than they had to begin with. Considering he'd been sorely distracted on several fronts during their exchanges, it would likely have taken a sword waved in his face to distract his attention away from Lady Julianna.

Lord knew, thoughts of her had diverted him from his purpose. Even now, when he should have paused after waking only long enough to inventory his aches and determine how best to get himself free of this place, what had he done? He'd lain upon his pallet as though he were at his leisure, daydreaming about a woman. He *had* gone soft! He had information to gather, he needed to find a mount so he could go on with his journey. He had to deliver the letters as soon as he could—

The letters!

Damn him for a mindless dolt! What had she done with them after he'd swooned? He didn't know which one she'd been reading when he'd caught her with them before, but none of them were intended for *her*. In the case of several of the missives, Will himself wasn't sure precisely what they were about. Nor did he wish to know, if truth be told.

By the rood, he carried messages from Lord Rannulf for the earl of Pembroke, information that could be vital to the defense of England and the protection of her king. He *had* to get them back and be on his way.

Heart racing, cursing himself for his foolishness, Will closed his eyes and pulled himself to his feet. One hand propped on the wall, he gathered himself and straightened, waiting for the wave of dizziness to pass before he dared move.

"Here now, milord!" Dora cried. "I doubt this is wise." The stool thumped against the floor. "Sit down before you fall again. Do you wish to undo all my mistress's care with your foolishness?"

Will opened his eyes. Dora stood on the other side of the pallet from him—eyes wide, hands on her hips, the stool on its side behind her—but she made no move toward him.

For which he was immensely grateful. 'Twould be embarrassing indeed if he was so weak an old woman could stop him, and if she couldn't, he'd no desire to harm her, either.

But leave this chamber he would, and under his own power.

The sensation that the room was swirling around him had stopped, and his legs had steadied enough to try them out. Keeping his palm flat against the wall, he started walking.

Though the chamber was small, the distance from his bed to the doorway loomed large before him. He moved with great care, all his attention focused on the solid oak planks that were his goal.

Dora screeched something at him, but he paid her words no heed. Sweat trickled down his brow and dripped onto his chest; Will placed one foot in front of the other until he could rest his forehead on the cool plaster wall beside the door.

The portal swung open, narrowly missing his shoulder. He simply glanced up, more intent upon marshalling his strength than on who was there.

Lady Julianna took one look at him, hastened into the room and slammed the door shut. The thud it made echoed through his head and threatened to send him reeling to the floor. He opened his mouth to protest—

"What in God's name are you doing?" she demanded of him, looking him square in the eyes. 'Twas clear her temper was in full bloom; her face had reddened and her voice sounded strange, higher than usual and a bit uneven. Will leaned weakly against the wall and made the mistake of shaking his head, though she scarce appeared to notice. He thought to answer her, then changed his mind.

Might as well save his breath for more important things, such as remaining on his feet and keeping his composure.

She scarcely looked at him anyway, instead turning her attention to the maid. "Dora, I leave you to watch over him and the next thing I know, he's out of bed and walking around!" she chided. "You assured me you'd take good care of him. By the Virgin, he was feverish and rambling in his sleep but a short time ago."

Rambling? Had he been delirious? He'd had strange dreams, 'twas true, especially ones involving Lady Julianna...

Jesu save him, he hoped hadn't said or tried to do any of the things he'd dreamed of!

If he had, he doubted he'd be standing here, he reassured himself. Most likely Lady Julianna would have crippled him.

Arms folded, she made a sound of disgust. "I thought I could trust you to keep him quiet and let him rest." She unfolded her arms and gestured toward him. "Have you gone as mad as he? Has he bewitched you, that you would stand there and permit him to wander out of here in such a state?" She took a step closer to the maid. "You know better than to—"

"How could Dora keep me in bed if I chose to

leave it?'' Will pointed out. When he asked the question, Lady Julianna turned her attention back to him. He pushed away from the wall and faced her squarely. He felt fine, stronger than but a moment earlier—perhaps the foul draught Dora gave him had already done its work. Behind them, Dora squawked something, but they both ignored her. ''She couldn't keep me abed if she tried! Look at her, she's but a tiny bit of a thing! She scarce reaches my shoulder.''

''*Did* she try to stop you?''

''She spoke to me, aye—told me not to get up—but what else could she do? 'Twould be foolish for her to try anything more than that.'' He didn't doubt he could have sent the frail old woman flying across the room even in his present condition, had he been so ill-natured. ''Not that I'd have harmed her had she done anything more.''

''Then you're both mad,'' Lady Julianna stated with conviction.

''Why is that?'' Will asked. He wished she'd get to the point, for despite his renewed sense of strength, he knew not how long 'twould keep him on his feet.

Lady Julianna leaned down and snatched a

crumpled drying cloth from a pile on the floor. Grinning, she swept her gaze over him as she handed it to him. ''Because, Sir William, you're stark naked.''

Chapter Nine

Muttering a curse, Will jerked the piece of linen from Julianna and attempted to wrap it about his waist. The ends didn't quite meet, she noted, but it covered the most important parts.

Unfortunately.

Evidently he felt little embarrassment about his state of dishabille, however, for he met her gaze squarely, lips quirked into a slightly mocking smile as he pushed away from the wall and walked past her. Mary save her, but he was a temptation....

Nonetheless, his pale face and the shadow of pain in his eyes hinted that sheer determination alone kept him on his feet.

Dora continued to rant in the background, more or less ignored by Julianna—as was often the case when Dora was in this state. With Will as a distraction, 'twas all she could do to keep from pushing the woman out the door without a moment's hesitation—though what she'd do once she and Will were alone was a mystery to her. As the gist of Dora's tirade became clear, however, she forced her attention back to the maid.

"Enough, Dora!" Julianna cautioned. She regretted her sharp manner as soon as the words left her mouth, and she could see the hurt in the old woman's wrinkled face. She softened her tone. "I'm mistress of this holding now, a woman grown—not a child within your care any longer. I'll not be ordered from my own chambers for any reason. Sir William has not offended me, I assure you."

Far from it, though she'd no intention of sharing that fact with either of them.

Moving nearer to the petite woman, Julianna gently enveloped her in her arms. "Let me deal with this, please," she whispered as she held the maid close for a moment.

Dora returned the gesture and stepped back, veil and wimple askew—the usual result of Julianna's embrace. "Aye, milady," she replied with a solemn nod. "I was only saying what your own lady mother would have done. I swore to her I'd protect you—"

"Dora." Julianna held up her hand, the gesture—and the fierce look that went with it—effectively cutting off Dora's oft-repeated refrain. She'd no intention of allowing Dora to work herself into a tizzy—as she'd done too many times in the past—over what a proper lady should and should not do. Dora's strictures were prompted by love for both Lady Marian and Julianna. Allowing them to continue would serve no purpose but to inflame Julianna's impatience with the well-intentioned old woman.

A resigned expression passed fleetingly over Dora's face, followed by an avid glance at Will. She leaned closer to Julianna and whispered, "Indeed, milady, how could you help but look? He *is* a fine figure of a man, don't you think?"

Julianna heard a muffled laugh from Will. Evidently his head wound hadn't affected his hearing—not that Dora's attempt at a whisper was difficult to hear, at any rate. She wondered what he thought about Dora's comment, but fought the temptation to glance his way to see—lest he notice her agreement with Dora's assessment echoed in her own expression.

Instead, she reached down and twitched Dora's head covering back into place, smiling as she carried out the familiar act. "Dora, don't you start your nonsense now." She gave in to temptation and added, not bothering to lower her voice—which shook with amusement, "Wait until he's stronger, at least. Otherwise you're apt to frighten him witless."

"You might be surprised, milady," Dora replied in her normal tone. She gave Julianna a gentle nudge in the ribs before stepping away, the mischievous glint in her eyes at odds with her innocent expression. "Though I'm thinking—" she glanced at Will, her expression admiring "—he didn't look too upset to be standing before *you* in all the glory the good Lord gave him."

She smoothed down her gown and slipped past Julianna to the door. Hand on the latch, she turned and dropped a curtsey. "It's most definitely been a pleasure to meet you, Sir William," she said, her voice nigh a purr and a teasing smile brightening her face. "And to see you, well...."

"Dora," Julianna cautioned, giving the maid a stern glare.

"Adieu, Lady Julianna. Until later, Sir William,'' Dora added with a nod before she left, closing the door quietly behind her.

Julianna shook her head at the old woman's inconsistent standards. Those Dora claimed defined a lady's morals and behavior seemed oppressive and boring, while those she applied to herself were a bit too bold for Julianna's taste.

Her own standards fell somewhere in between the two extremes.

''Milady,'' Will interrupted her thoughts. ''Am I confused and feverish again, or did I notice that old woman flirting with me?''

Julianna shifted to face him. He'd moved to stand near the narrow window slit, a blanket knotted loosely about his hips and covering him to his ankles, one arm resting along the edge of the stone embrasure. She buried her disappointment that he'd wrapped up as much as he had; she far preferred his earlier garb, brief as it had been, she thought, suppressing a mischievous smile.

''Nay, she was serious,'' she told him solemnly as she joined him. Seeing him in the bright light streaming through the opening, she realized he'd likely taken up his relaxed stance against the wall by the window for support, and to disguise the fact that he was ready to collapse. His blond hair fell in disarray to his shoulders, which drooped with weariness. His face beneath several days' growth of beard was haggard and pale. She sighed. If she were to unwind the bandages covering his wounds, she'd likely find them spotted with blood again.

"Lady Julianna." Evidently he felt well enough to stand there talking, or wished to appear so.

Why hadn't he returned to his pallet at once after Dora had left them, instead of carrying out this pretense that he was strong enough to be on his feet, standing about the chamber?

What a ridiculous question, Julianna! Had the sight of Will scrambled her wits still more? What man would take to his pallet if he could manage to prop himself upright? Never mind that he'd be back in that bed—and feverish again, no doubt—before much more time passed. She'd do him no favor by keeping him here talking.

But how to convince him to return to bed?

"Milady? Are you well?"

Why wouldn't she be?

"Julianna?" At his questioning look, she nodded. "Aye, of course. I was simply…distracted by the thought of some tasks I neglected.'' Distracted, yes—by him, in every way.

Mayhap he was tired of lying abed, and the warm sun shining on him had to feel good. If he began to topple over, she'd simply have to catch him.

Again.

Wouldn't that be a hardship? she asked herself mockingly.

Would the blanket remain in place if he fell?

Sweet Mary, what was wrong with her? She should spend an entire day and night on her knees in the chapel, praying for forgiveness for the sin of lust.

Such penitence would mean little, however, if she didn't regret her lecherous thoughts.

Regret them? Amusement sent a bubble of laughter from her lips. Nay, she relished every one.

She peeked at him from beneath her lashes—his muscular chest and arms exposed, their dusting of dark blond curls a temptation she could scarce ignore; his blond hair tousled, his bewhiskered face giving him the look of temptation personified. Nay, 'twas not regret making her heart beat faster and her flesh burn for more than a mere glimpse of him.

Nay, this was lust. And if it was a sin to feel this way, then she'd be damned for it; she intended to enjoy every moment of it—even if all she did was imagine what 'twould be like to lie with him. 'Twould be worth a thousand "Our Fathers" or whatever penance she must perform.

Will touched her shoulder briefly with his hand, startling her from her reverie and sending a wave of heat rushing up to color her cheeks at the lurid bent of her thoughts. "Lady Julianna, are you all right?" He watched her closely, his blue eyes far too perceptive for her comfort.

"O-of course," she stammered. *He cannot see what is in your mind, Julianna,* she chided herself. *Thank goodness.*

Drawing a calming breath, she caged her wayward thoughts and tucked them away for further contemplation later. "About Dora... Truly, I'm sure she meant what she said. Though she wouldn't want me to tell you outright, Dora does enjoy men."

Will snorted and his eyes lit with amusement. "That much is obvious! But she's *old*—"

"As she's fond of saying, she may be old, but

she's not dead. Nor is she blind.'' Julianna chuckled. ''I doubt she said a single word to warn you of your state of undress, did she?''

''If she had, I'd not have been parading about in front of her—or you—without covering myself with something first,'' he assured her.

Thank you, Dora, for your "restraint."

Julianna smiled. ''I'll wager she's already gone upstairs to the solar to gossip with her friends, describing you to them in glorious detail, all of them spinning tales about their past adventures as fast as they spin wool.''

An expression of horror crossed his face. ''You don't think she really believes I'd be...interested in her, do you?''

''Most likely she doesn't,'' she assured him. ''If she thought you were a likely target, she'd have tried much harder to fix your interest. And if she was serious, she'd not have teased you about your garb...or lack of it. Not in front of me.''

''I certainly wouldn't have stood there in front of you in all my 'glory,' as Dora put it, had I realized I was stark naked, either.'' His lips curved into a teasing smile, and a hint of challenge brightened his blue eyes. "At least not till we've come to know each other a little better."

"That would have been a shame," she couldn't resist saying, "for most assuredly 'twas a sight to brighten any maiden's day."

Was that her voice, so low and intimate? She hadn't known she could sound like that!

"I thank you, milady," he said with a nod. He leaned toward her, closing the distance between them. A tempting smile brightened his face and made her heart beat faster. "'Tis every knight's desire to gratify a fair maid." He reached out, pushed an errant wisp of dark hair back from her cheek and tucked it gently behind her ear, his fingers lingering on the sensitive skin of her neck for a moment. "I'm honored to have pleased you." His hand slipped forward to cup her face. "'Twould be *my* pleasure to please you more," he added, his voice as much a caress as his feathery touch.

She could feel the warmth of his body, smell the scent she already recognized as Will's. Though she knew she should move away, her traitorous body refused to obey her mind's command.

Instead she moved nearer to him, her mouth softening for the brush of his lips. She returned the faint pressure, savoring the slight rasp of his whiskers on her chin as he bent over her and trailed his tongue over the seam of her mouth before he covered her lips for a more drawn-out kiss.

Heat filled her, sensitizing her flesh and making her bold. Throwing all caution to the wind, Julianna brought her hands up to cup Will's face, and gave herself over to the joy of desire freely shared.

Chapter Ten

His lips were cool and tasted of mint and spring water, Julianna noted absently, but heat radiated from him where their bodies pressed together. She smoothed her hands over his cheeks and jaw, as much because she couldn't help but savor the brush of his beard-roughened face against the sensitive skin of her palms as to check for fever. Her flesh tingled from the subtle caress, but she wrenched her focus to Will, the injured warrior—though her sense of him purely as male to her female nigh threatened to overwhelm her judgment.

She felt no hint of fever on his face…a relief, after the past few days.

And a pleasure as well, she considered—could

it be that he burned with the same fire that smoldered through her veins?

The thought alone made her heart leap within her breast and set her pulse pounding harder.

Did he feel the same desire—one that sharpened her senses, made her yearn to cast aside a lifetime's worth of caution?

Oh, how she hoped he did!

He slipped his hand along her neck and cupped her nape beneath her braid, burying his fingers in her hair. There was no weakness in his touch; Will's hold, though gentle, revealed the power of the muscular arms wrapped securely about her.

Julianna drew a shuddering breath and released it slowly. She found the contrast of strength and tenderness stimulating—nigh overwhelming—and savored every nuance of it. His lips urged her to madness, a compulsion she could not help but obey.

Will fought the insistent drive to grab at Julianna, to thrust her up against the wall and press his aching flesh into her softness until they both found sweet release. His body had not yet cooled from the passionate dreams of her that had haunted his restless sleep; the reality of her in his arms made his hurts and woes naught but a memory too weak to regard.

Instead he concentrated on Julianna—took his time, kept his kiss slow and measured, a deliberate act intended to draw her into the same heightened awareness that held him captured within its spell.

At first she didn't seem to know what to do with her hands. She rested them on his shoulders, her touch hesitant, tentative, not at all what he craved. He caught her hands in his and placed them at his waist, holding them there until her tension eased.

Will sucked in a shaky breath and rested his forehead on her cheek as she touched him of her own volition. Her hands were strong and sure on the sensitive flesh of his stomach, the burst of pleasure she engendered nigh sending him to his knees.

Eyes closed, he cradled her face with his hands for a moment and savored the sensation. Once he had his body under control once more, he raised his head and stared into her eyes. She stared back at him, the amber in her eyes turned to deep gold. She looked drugged with pleasure, and a glint of curiosity lightened her gaze.

"Did I hurt you?" Julianna asked sharply. She jerked her hands away from him and held them out to her sides, the movement putting a mere handbreadth of distance between them.

A mere handbreadth...yet it was too far.

He stroked her jaw with his fingertips and twisted his lips into a wry smile. The loss of contact with her sent an ache through him as painful in its way as the wounds that still throbbed beneath his bandages. "Only when you moved away," he murmured.

She put her hand out and, her touch tentative, brushed her fingers carefully along his uninjured arm. "I'm sorry, I didn't realize—"

"'Twas not a physical pain, Julianna," he assured her. "You didn't harm me." Though he wanted to move her hands back to him, he restrained himself; he'd far prefer a caress freely given. Instead he buried his fingers into her hair and tugged the wavy strands free of the loose braid. He gave a wry smile. "'Twas the sense of loss I felt when you took your hands from me. Will you touch me again?"

"If 'tis your desire." Her gaze considering, she watched his face while she rested her palms on his stomach. "If you're certain it won't cause you any further hurt, Will."

"Nay, I'm fine." Only a mortal wound could keep him from this play. Curious as to what she'd do next, he simply stood and watched her, hoping she'd not turn timid now.

Amusement—mixed with a tinge of curiosity—lit her face as she slipped her fingers lingeringly over the ridged muscles of his belly, then slid them to his waist, drawing out the teasing motion till he thought he'd go mad. The movement *almost* brought their lower bodies into contact again, and made the blanket knotted at his hips sink a bit lower.

He doubted 'twould slide off, however—not with his arousal tenting the soft wool fabric in a most obvious manner.

Her expression a challenge, Julianna took advantage of the additional exposed flesh and dragged her nails through the hair curling about his navel.

Will bit back a most unholy plea to the Virgin Mother. "If I told you all I desire of you at this moment, milady—" he shifted his legs and widened his stance, settling himself against her and trapping her hands—and his arousal—between them ''—you would likely flee this chamber as swiftly as you could go.''

She smiled and made no effort to free her hands or to move away. ''You cannot believe me to be so fainthearted.'' The faint scent of flowers he already associated with Julianna intensified as he combed through the tousled mass to the ends, the fragrance of roses and lavender a heady complement to the sensation of her hair brushing his skin. He shuddered. ''You are so very lovely, milady,'' he whispered. ''A warrior goddess fit to send a man to his knees before you.''

She held his gaze warily at his words, then seemed to ease her vigilance. Her smile widened and rosy color tinted her cheeks. ''Now there's a vision fit to gladden a lady's heart.'' Her voice was low, and shook with amusement...and something more?

Was it desire that made him hear passion in her words, when she spoke?

The mere sound of her voice made his manhood swell with want of her, while the image her words brought forth to fill his mind's eye sent his pulse racing. Her body settled against him more fully, bringing her flush with him from waist to knees. ''Let me...'' He drank of her smooth, full lips, the tentative brush of her tongue at the corner of his mouth sending his heart soaring.

Julianna swept her hands from between them and up over his chest, halting when she reached the band of linen wrapped about his wound. "I wish you'd never come to harm, Will." She bent and traced her lips along his collarbone, a caress meant to soothe—though it nigh sent Will to his knees. Sighing, she added, "Though then we'd never have met."

Shouts rose from beneath the window, blended with the shrill sound of women's voices raised in disagreement. Bleating sheep and squealing pigs added to the chaos, the noise pushing apart Will and Julianna as effectively as a cold downpour.

Eyes downcast, Julianna took a step back and leaned out the open window. "What—" Her voice, scratchy and weak, broke on the word. Will placed a hand on her shoulder, wanting to ease her from the fire of passion to the intrusion of the day-to-day world. He rubbed her back soothingly, but she ignored the supportive caress, cleared her throat and drew a deep breath. "What is going on down there?" she shouted. "Be silent and stay put, the lot of you! I'll be down in a trice."

Standing out of sight behind her, Will eased

Julianna back into the room far enough that her passion-flushed face wouldn't be apparent to the crowd assembled below. He'd seen calmer mêlées at a tournament, but no doubt the vision of their mistress in such obvious disarray would capture their attention faster than if he'd fired a flaming arrow into their midst.

He gathered Julianna's tumbled hair together and swept it over her shoulders. "Wait a bit before you leave, milady, else 'twill be all too clear to them what we've been about."

She laughed, a weak sound with little of amusement about it. "Of course. We wouldn't want them to know their lady has been acting the lightskirt."

Will reached out and caught her by the chin. "Nay, Julianna." He captured her gaze with his, waning her to see the truth of his words. "Not a lightskirt—a noble lady. A desirable woman."

"Noble ladies—" She made a derisive sound. "*Women* don't—"

Will's chuckle cut her off. "Aye, love, they do. Once you've settled this conflict, I'd be happy to tell you—or show you—precisely what women and men do," he offered. "Noble or otherwise."

He was glad to note that as he'd intended, his words brought a glint of true humor to her eyes.

An uneasy silence reigned in the bailey, but he doubted 'twould last much longer. Staying a few paces back from the window, he drew her near to press a kiss to her brow before stepping aside and giving her shirt a tug to straighten it. "Here, Julianna, now you're fit for public view, with none the wiser that their warrior lady is also a woman of passion."

She crossed the room, then paused by the door and glanced over her shoulder at him. Her cheeks were still flushed, Will noted, but from his words, not the residual of desire. He couldn't mistake the teasing look she sent him. "Perhaps I am," she agreed. "But I fear we must discuss the topic at another time." Sending him a smile he could only describe as flirtatious, she turned and left the chamber, closing the door behind her with a snap.

Chapter Eleven

When Julianna approached the crowd of women and several men gathered in the bailey, she felt as though everyone could see exactly what she and Will had been doing upstairs. Indeed, she'd swear she could still feel the imprint of Will's body against hers, while the heat of passion generated by their kisses made her all too aware of her body in a way she'd never been before—a way that she recognized as feminine, a woman's recognition of man, of the need to mate.

Nay, Julianna, you weren't standing that close to the window. No one saw you. 'Tis guilt alone making you feel as though your every thought and action are written plain upon your face—and your body—for all to observe.

Nonetheless she reached for the strings lacing

the neck of her shirt, tying them into a firm knot in the hope of hiding the tide of heat she felt moving up her throat to her face at the mere thought of Will. Thankfully she'd bound her breasts snugly with the linen band, else her thin shirt would likely have made their recent—and unceasing—alertness quite apparent. Unfortunately recalling the evidence of Will's own "alertness" made her body heat more.

She'd not calm herself by thinking of him, 'twas certain!

Pausing a moment on the fringe of grass encircling the dusty bailey, she sought to collect herself; if she kept on in this manner, she'd soon be as mindless and coy as a giddy maid! She'd seen it happen often enough. A bare hint of attention from a man and the woman suddenly became a simpering ninny, unable to think, to perform the simplest tasks....

Until recently, she'd never have believed 'twould be a difficulty *she* would be forced to endure.

For her, 'twas a state to be avoided at all costs. She dared not succumb to any man's temptation, if that would be the result!

"Lady Julianna!" a woman cried from within

the group gathered before her. Jolted from her reverie, Julianna noted that the mob had begun to grow restive while she hesitated, though she knew she'd not stood there for too long with her mind wandering.

Still, they'd begun to shift restlessly, muttering amongst themselves, though they'd not yet returned to their previous din. However, the expressions on some of the women's faces looked mean and angry. She'd best intervene now, before they had the chance to work themselves back into a frenzy.

With a skill born of practice, she settled her features into the face of command and approached the throng with confident strides. They parted readily enough to allow her into their midst, though their chatter took longer to fade away.

She waited till they quieted. "What's amiss?" she asked. "I cannot imagine what could account for such a commotion! By our Lady, a gaggle of geese on their way to the slaughter would have made less of a commotion than the lot of you."

One last person blocked her view of the center of attention—Diccon, one of the younger men-at-arms, stood fast, stubborn resolve written on his slender countenance. However, he obeyed when she motioned for him to move aside, leaving her face-to-face with Mary, the maid who had ignored Julianna's summons to help the night she'd brought Will to Tuck's Tower.

Mary's gown hung loose off one shoulder and was twisted about her generous body. Dust and muck streaked the faded wool, and her dirt-stained cheek bore the unmistakable mark of fresh horse dung, clods of which lay spattered on the ground around her. She clutched a small, crumpled bundle of fabric tight to her bosom, her pretty features drawn just as rigidly into an expression of fear. "Milady, please don't let 'em do any more! They were goin' to stone me 'less I leave Tuck's Tower this very day an' don't come back. I've done nothin' to 'em, and I got nowhere to go," she added before lowering her face into the mass of fabric and sobbing quietly.

"What is the meaning of this?" Julianna demanded, stepping nearer to the woman and lending her the protection of her authority. The crowd shifted until they faced Mary and Julianna, the men gathered off to one side, the women to the other. They'd arrayed themselves before her like two troops of combatants ready to do battle—no doubt an accurate assessment, to judge by their expressions.

Joan, one of the older kitchen maids, stepped forward. "We do want her gone from here, milady," she said, her jaw held at a challenging angle and her hands fisted upon her scrawny hips. "Today. She's up to no good, She's been nothin' but trouble since she got here, and it's past time we did somethin' about it."

Several of the other women in the crowd nodded their agreement, while two of the men standing near the front shifted their feet in the dust and wouldn't meet Julianna's gaze.

Though she assumed she knew where this conversation was headed, Julianna simply looked at them expectantly. "Is that so?"

"Aye, milady," Joan said with a decisive nod. "Up to no good she is—we've known that from the time she came here. 'Tis common knowledge."

"What does 'up to no good' mean?" Julianna asked, biting back a groan of aggravation. Why must they decide to fight each other now, when lack of sleep had deprived her of any patience to deal with them?

Hadn't they anything else to do to occupy

themselves? Fields to tend, weapons to repair, animals to care for? Lord knew she'd tasks enough! "Have you caught Mary stealing? Fouling our well? Poisoning our sheep?" She placed her hand on her knife hilt and took a step forward; Joan's tone and attitude were so self-righteous that the old besom deserved to feel the threat of her mistress's annoyance. "Have you found her consorting with our enemies?"

Mary moaned and huddled more deeply into the bundle of cloth.

"Nay, not our enemies, Lady Julianna," another of the women cried. "'Tis our men! She's been consortin' wi' our sweethearts, the sneakin' harlot. From the time that strumpet came wigglin' her arse through the gates, she's done nothin' but tease 'em an' toy with 'em till she has her way. Now that they've got *her* to see to 'em whenever they want, they'll have nothin' to do wi' decent women," she added, her voice rising to an annoying whine.

The other women seemed to take this as their cue to all air their grievances at once, making it impossible for Julianna to understand their words, though their meaning was clear enough. "Is that so?" She didn't attempt to hide her disdain at so ridiculous a claim. While she herself had always considered Mary to be a shameless wench, she doubted any woman had the desire—or the vigor—to bed so many men!

Nor could she bed them all at once.

Could she?

Julianna thrust that disquieting thought aside and turned to Mary. Whatever the woman had been doing with the men, 'twas doubtful she deserved to be stoned and cast from their gates—Julianna's prior angry thoughts about the maid's behavior notwithstanding.

She laid her hand on the woman's shoulder, still aquiver from her crying. "Here now, we'll not resolve anything with you hiding away, Mary. Straighten up and show your face. They'll not harm you while I'm here to protect you."

"But what about when you're gone, milady?" Mary spoke quietly, not bothering to do more than slightly lift her head. "They'll only wait until later, then find some other way to get me. They always do."

The maid's calm tone made it clear she expected nothing different. What must it be like to simply presume you'd be abused, to accept that abuse as though it was your due? As the beloved daughter of Tuck's Tower, no one had ever dared threaten Julianna personally, and while she'd not always had her way, she'd found it an annoyance, nothing more serious than that.

"Nay—we'll put an end to this right now," Julianna told her, her tone firm.

Mary raised her head. Tears had smeared the filth on her face, making her appear even more messy and miserable than before. She seemed to have folded in upon herself as well, becoming a vulnerable and confused child-woman brought to face an angry mob, rather than the aggressive rebel Julianna had assumed her to be from her previous actions.

"Come, calm yourself." Julianna snatched at the trailing corner of Mary's bundle and carefully wiped at the dust and filth smearing the maid's face. The simple action seemed to startle Mary so much that she remained motionless until Julianna finished.

Not so a mottled blotch marred Mary's smooth skin, Julianna marveled, and Mary's eyes, tear-dewed though they were, bore no trace of red from her crying. Especially compared to the angry women facing them, Mary did appear a sight to tempt a man. 'Twas easy to see why the others resented her—for her looks alone!—whether or not she'd done what they accused her of.

"Thank ye, milady," Mary whispered. She squared her shoulders and straightened as Julianna had bid her. Evidently heartened by her mistress's support, the maid smiled. 'Twas a wobbly attempt, but at least the wench had ceased her crying, Julianna noted wryly. Mary drew in a deep breath, an act which made her bosom threaten to spill from her loose bodice, and elevated her gaze, and her chin, in a challenging pose. She tugged her gown into place and fixed her stare on the group of women.

"No more sniveling or whining," Julianna warned. "Or accusations, either. We cannot all stand about wasting time." She glanced at the two factions, not bothering to hide her displeasure. "Let's put an end to this here and now, so we can all go about our business."

Diccon stepped a little away from his fellows and cleared his throat. "Don't ye worry none, Mary. We'll see to it they leave ye alone, just like we always do." He glanced around the group, his gaze lingering on Joan and another, slightly younger woman who stood nearby. They glared back at him. "The miserable old witches are just jealous o' you, 'tis all."

Interesting. Julianna hadn't considered that there could be any other reason for Mary to spend most of her time in the men's barracks besides the obvious one that she was spreading her... favors...among the men.

She doubted 'twas as innocent as the young soldier made it sound, though after Diccon had spent the past few years training and living with the rough lot of men-at-arms who made up her guard, she didn't imagine him to be an innocent, either.

Especially as he'd grown up in the village among the earthy and opinionated survivors of her father's old band of outlaws.

He turned to Julianna, his expression so earnest she immediately revised her previous assumption. "We been keepin' an eye on her, milady, so's they'll leave her be. At least wi' us she's safe from their pinchin' and proddin' and spiteful ways." He pointed to the bandage tied about his upper arm, the white linen vivid against the sleeve of his grimy brown jerkin. "In return, she fixes us up when we need it."

"I'll wager she 'fixes' *ye* all right, Diccon," a woman in the back of the group quipped.

"Though I don't imagine the hurt she fixes is anything ye'd want a bandage tied 'round.' O' course, I could be wrong."

That conjured up an interesting image in Julianna's mind, though the man her imagination brought forth was tall, blond and handsome—and had nothing whatsoever to do with Diccon. Still, the remark had been funny; she bit back a snort of amusement, for she doubted 'twould serve for her to join in the chorus of laughter that met *that* observation.

Still, she couldn't help but be glad of the comment, for even some of the women appeared distracted from their previous fury.

Julianna realized who'd spoken, for she recognized the voice. 'Twas Trudy, a laundry maid well-known for her wit. Not surprisingly, humor had brightened Trudy's voice; Julianna had never seen her without a smile on her face. Why the usually merry woman had joined the outraged gathering was a mystery, however.

Diccon's face reddened, but he laughed. "Ye never do know, Trudy," he replied. "Though we most likely shouldn't be talking like this in front of Lady Julianna. Beg pardon, milady."

His words made her feel almost an interloper.

A sudden need to be gone beset her; it began to seem as though they'd stood here in the bailey forever. She'd no patience left to act as mediator, or for much else, if truth be told.

Julianna glanced around, taking note of the stable boys raking the bare ground as they sought to appear busy while watching the commotion. Peering up, she saw a cluster of weavers at the wide window of the solar. The women stood packed together as tight as the threads they should have been weaving, staring avidly down into the bailey rather than working productively at their looms.

Her annoyance mounting, she shifted her gaze to the window below the solar, where she could see that Will had remained a part of their audience as well.

For some reason that fact forced her temper from impatient to foul.

"Mary, Joan, Diccon, Trudy—come with me." She snapped out the words, her sharp tone eliciting a few startled looks. "As for the rest of you, I'm sure you've better things to do. I suggest you go and do them." Julianna barely paused to be certain they'd obeyed her before turning on her heel and heading for the stairs leading into the hall.

* * *

She led the four of them into a small chamber off to the side of the hall, closing the door with an uncharacteristic snap. The sound jarred her from the fog of edginess and annoyance dogging her, bringing with it an embarrassed sense that she'd suddenly begun to behave like an impatient brat.

What was wrong with her? she wondered as she crossed the room and eased herself onto the wide seat beneath the window. She'd always had a temper—who did not, after all? But she'd not been one to inflict her ill humor on others, nor to treat her people so poorly as she feared she just had done. Guilt rising, she motioned for the others to sit on the bench alongside the wall facing her.

They positioned themselves just as Julianna expected; Diccon and Trudy in the middle, with Joan on one side of them, Mary on the other.

Hopeful that this arrangement indicated that no additional fighting would take place for the moment, Julianna closed her eyes, dragged a hand through her hair and worked to regain her good sense.

"Milady, are you all right?" Diccon asked.

Before Julianna's weary and confused brain

could conjure up an answer for him, a burst of laughter made her eyes pop open.

"Of course she's not, you dolt!" Trudy jabbed her elbow into Diccon's side. "'Tis clear enough to *me*. Can't you see what's ailin' her?"

"Enough o' that, wench." Diccon moved Trudy a handbreadth away with a gentle nudge. "See what? You don't *look* sick, milady," he assured Julianna with what was no doubt meant to be encouragement.

"I didn't say she was sick," Trudy told him, winking. "Ailing, I said. 'Tis not the same at all, if you know what I mean."

Julianna *didn't* know what Trudy meant—nor did the others, judging by their bewildered expressions.

Trudy sighed, leapt to her feet and swept her hand toward her mistress. "'Tis that man," she said. "The handsome knight our own warrior lady carried here, across her saddlebow, like in the old legends," she added. "Don't you all see? Lady Julianna is in love! Our Bride of the Tower is about to become a wife in truth."

Chapter Twelve

From his vantage point by the window, Will observed the scene in the bailey, his interest piqued when Julianna hung back for a moment before joining the others. Why did she hesitate to jump into the fray? The crowd seemed to be made up of servants and a few men-at-arms—surely nothing of much concern to her. Besides, he didn't imagine his warrior lady feared much of anything.

In truth, he didn't know much about Tuck's Tower, definitely not enough to know if how Julianna managed it could account for her reluctance. So instead he allowed himself to hope her reason for waiting there had something to do with him.

Will could only imagine what Gillian might say to that! ''Arrogant knave,'' she'd call him, accompanied by a poke in the chest and a shake of her head, most likely. The fact that she was the lady of l'Eau Clair, a wife and mother, didn't keep her from reverting to their childhood behavior when she felt that circumstances warranted. Will scratched at his bewhiskered chin and chuckled. She'd be right—it *was* an arrogant thought.

Though he'd never before considered himself an exceptionally arrogant man, the attention of a woman like Julianna was apt to make him so.

In his own defense, however, how could any man, having encountered Julianna, not seek to capture her interest?

Or feel damned proud of himself—become cocksure indeed, he thought, groaning at his feeble jest—to have attained it?

As he watched her interact with the irate mob, to his eyes she seemed impatient, annoyed. Now that no one was shouting, the voices had faded to a mere buzz of sound. He couldn't hear what was going on down there, but no doubt something they'd said had caused her to appear ready to bolt at the slightest provocation.

Or perhaps she hadn't yet been ready to leave *him,* not quite willing to end the enticing give and take they'd scarcely begun to explore. Lord knew *he* felt annoyed—nay, more than that, *aggravated*—that they had been so abruptly interrupted.

Could it be he'd had as much of an effect upon her as she'd had on him?

He had never reacted to any woman with the driving sense of need that he felt when he held Julianna in his arms!

His injuries nigh forgotten, Will folded his arms and leaned back against the wooden frame surrounding the window. He'd much rather focus his interest on the lovely woman who had so easily captured his....

His what? His attention, of a certainty, mind and body both. There was something about Lady Julianna d'Arcy that held his interest, his thoughts, far too easily for his peace of mind.

Lust he was familiar with, 'twas straightforward, understood by any man.

Or so he'd believed. 'Twas easy to recognize his body's aching need for a woman, for the ease satisfying that ache could bring.

Yet despite his desire for Julianna, a craving far stronger than any he had felt before, he didn't believe that a simple coupling with her could come close to satisfying his need.

Nor did he feel the slightest urge to fulfill that

desire with any other woman. It wasn't that he wanted a woman, he realized, staring down at the light glinting off her shining hair.

He wanted *her*.

Will allowed his thoughts to dwell on the startling idea, surprised that it caused him no panic or fear—no sense of discomfort at all. In truth, he recognized with a startling sense of certainty that Julianna might be the woman he would never tire of.

How that could be, he had no notion.

While the concept of one woman for a man— *the* woman—each attached to the other with ties more binding and constant than those of squire to knight, vassal to overlord—might be unusual, he was aware of the concept. Will had seen that sort of relationship firsthand, several times in fact. Between Lord Rannulf and Lady Gillian, of course, as well as with others in Gillian's family; they did seem to be a faithful lot. And most recently during his time in Ireland, for none could mistake the ties of love and devotion uniting Connor Fitz-Clifford, Rannulf's twin, to Lady Moira, his Irish bride.

Now that he considered it, nigh every couple

within Lady Gillian's milieu had been stricken with that particular ailment.

Was he next?

Whatever had caused him to believe he was about to embark on *that* lunacy?

He didn't know Julianna well enough to feel anything more than desire for her. By the rood, he knew next to nothing about her. She was lovely, brave and unusual. Although he'd met women who possessed those same characteristics, he'd never felt driven to recklessness by the mere scent of their hair.

He'd be a fool to forget the plans he'd made for his future. He'd already progressed far in his strategy for establishing and improving his place in the world. His approach didn't include a doomed-from-the-start liaison with a woman so clearly above his station.

Despite his ambition, he was the son of a simple archer. Knight though he'd become, he knew better than to aim his bolt so high as that!

'Twas a sure way to lose everything he'd worked for, perhaps even his life, depending upon Julianna's connections of blood or fealty.

Not to mention that he knew nothing of what Julianna might feel for him. While a lady could—

and often did—desire a simple knight, she'd no reason to do anything more than to bed him to satisfy that inclination. He understood that well enough. 'Twas arrogant indeed for him to assume anything more.

He knew what he felt must be a form of madness, irrational and apparently haphazard.

Why didn't that fact concern him?

Whatever it was that Julianna made him feel was completely foreign to his own experience. He wanted her, of course, but he also believed she'd be a captivating companion, a distraction from life's trials, a fellow warrior to share tales of battle.

Now there was a thought to strike fear in the heart of a man of war! Had the fact that one of the fellow "warriors" of his childhood had been female altered his view of the world? After growing up with Lady Gillian—back when she'd called herself Gilles and dressed in the same boy's clothing as he—Julianna's choice of garb, and her penchant for arming herself with a fighter's gear as she went about her business, didn't strike him as odd.

She seemed an extremely capable woman, well trained to care for herself and her people...well suited to care for him, a tempting voice in his mind added.

What would it be like to know that care? To be the center of her notice, to have the intensity of her affection, her attention, focused solely upon him?

He leaned his hands on the window frame and stretched, the pain in his arm a mere twinge in comparison to the emotions pouring through him.

The effect of those feelings struck him with the power of a lance, making his heart thunder in his chest and his stomach twist. Julianna was nigh a stranger to him; how could his reaction to her be so strong?

Mayhap 'twas naught but the effect of that noxious draught Dora had forced upon him, he reassured himself, nothing more. Something about it had played havoc with his brain, caused his thoughts to shift and swirl, made his pulse thunder and race.

Who knew what the old woman had put in it? he wondered with a touch of dread. She did seem a lusty wench, in spite of her years; perhaps she'd knowledge of some arcane art that could keep her supplied with bed partners. He'd heard stories of herbs that could compel a man to passion, potions to make him ache for satisfaction until he was driven to couple with the first woman he saw.

Could Dora have dosed him with something to spur on his lust? She'd believed she'd be alone with him a while, that much had been obvious from her surprise when Julianna had arrived. Recalling the comments—the insinuations she'd made—set his stomach roiling uneasily. What if she'd thought to have her way with him while they'd been alone together?

He'd just as soon avoid that scenario.

Reconsidering *all* that Dora had said and done before Julianna joined them, her good care of him and her obvious love for her mistress, sent a wave of shame rolling over him.

Jesu, but he must be losing his mind to even consider such a thing. Perhaps the fever had overheated his brain and made him susceptible to bizarre delusions.

Uncomfortable with that thought, instead he shifted his attention to Julianna once again. The sun made her hair glow, discovering the hints of reddish blond woven among the brown tresses. Her simple beauty shone in her honest face, her clear amber eyes, her forthright manner, independent of the usual female artifices. When he looked at her, he saw *Julianna,* not a woman tricked out in fine clothing and paint.

'Twas a pleasure simply to watch her.

However, he noticed her actions lacked her usual grace of movement as she swiped a bit of cloth over the face of a grimy woman who seemed to be the focus of the commotion. 'Twas a kind act, one he didn't believe many noble ladies would have made, nevertheless one he wasn't surprised to see Julianna perform. She'd nothing of haughtiness about her. Yet her expression and bearing revealed a tension about her at odds with her thoughtful gesture.

A flash of temper crossed her features, although something one of the men-at-arms said made a hint of amusement lighten her expression as the others laughed.

She looked weary, Will thought, and no wonder, if she'd remained by his side and nursed him through his fever and delusions. His recollection of that time might be vague and confusing, but Julianna didn't strike him as the kind of woman who would abandon him to his illness to take her rest.

Remorse filled him; he owed Lady Julianna his gratitude for his life, and his respect for her kindness and patience. He glanced down at the blanket drooping round his hips and dragging on the floor. Why hadn't he dressed as soon as she'd left, prepared himself to leave Tuck's Tower and return to his duties? He felt immeasurably better since he'd swallowed Dora's potion.

Nay, instead he'd stood there gawping at Lady Julianna like a lovesick lad, thinking thoughts about her that he had no business permitting to enter his mind. All in all, his behavior toward her had been disrespectful in the extreme.

He'd been taught better manners and duty both.

'Twas time to leave, to thank her and allow them both to get on with their lives and duties.

Ignoring the crowd, Lady Julianna looked about the bailey, then up at the windows. He recognized the moment she saw him standing there, for her expression darkened, and her words rang sharply through the bailey.

If she'd looked annoyed before, 'twas nothing to her bad humor now.

And it appeared he'd been at least partially the cause.

As soon as she passed from view, Will thrust aside the blanket and carefully made his way across the chamber. Aye, it could be a good opportunity for him to leave—now, while she had other things on her mind to distract her attention from him.

There was no time to waste, for he needed to discover what she'd done with his message pouch, find some way to slip into the stables for a horse and a weapon before he slipped out the gates with none the wiser.

He didn't know what he'd done to set off Lady Julianna's temper, but he didn't want to linger here too long to find out. He didn't dare give her any further chance to hold him here, not when he'd other places he had to be.

When Will stooped to pick up his clothes from the floor, he nigh toppled over onto his pallet. Determination fired him, however; he straightened, closed his eyes and waited till his head ceased whirling like a top before attempting to thread his legs into his braes and pull them up. His arm and shoulder were stiff and hurt like the devil, but he ignored the pain and managed to tug his shirt over his head before he had to sink down on the stool Dora left by the bed.

He sat there a long time, far longer than he liked, concentrating deeply. He breathed slowly and willed himself to calm, sought to regain his usual sense of purpose, if not of power. Eventually the strength returned to his legs and his head felt firmly attached to his neck once more.

Barefooted and barely dressed, Will scooped up his boots and tucked them under his arm. Moving silently, he made his way to the door Julianna had neglected to bolt. While it wasn't the one to her chamber, unfortunately—for he thought she might have stored his letters there—thankfully he had a way to leave the room without being forced to climb out the window and down the wall of the keep.

He pressed his ear against the stout oak panels and listened, but all was quiet without. He opened the door easily, the hinges making not a sound. He peeked through the narrow opening. Not a soul in sight.

Mouth curving into a faint smile of satisfaction, Will crept through the opening and out into the deserted hallway.

Chapter Thirteen

"...Lady Julianna is in love! Our Bride of the Tower is about to become a wife in truth."

Trudy's words echoed in Julianna's ears, making her breath seize in her chest before the obviously demented woman had finished uttering her absurd assumption. If Julianna hadn't been frozen in place, she'd have found a way to halt the flow of words before Trudy could finish saying them.

In truth, however, despite her earlier fears, she would never have expected to hear such a thing. Not from Trudy, at any rate. The laundry maid had never even *seen* Will!

Though Dora had, Julianna reminded herself. And she'd seen the two of them together. She bit back a groan. The old woman had wasted no time spreading her gossip, embellished to season the tale, too. Dora had clearly allowed her surprisingly romantic nature to overcome her sense.

This was all she needed, to remind everyone of the Bride story. 'Twas difficult enough at times for her to maintain command of the Tower and its inhabitants, without them seeking a mate for her so she could relinquish control of her home—and herself—to him.

Heat crept up her neck. She'd been a fool, she thought bitterly, to permit her guard to lapse for a moment. Evidently her desire for Will *had* been blatantly obvious.

Had it been worth the risk?

She didn't know.

She glanced from Trudy to the others. Julianna hadn't been the only person struck silent. Mary and Diccon both stared at Trudy; Diccon's expression amazed, Mary's derisive.

Since they weren't watching her, thankfully, Julianna took the opportunity to compose herself.

Trudy's excited smile began to fade. "Aren't ye happy for our lady?" she asked. "'Tis a wonderful thing! Dora says—"

"Dora says a lot of things," Mary pointed out, her voice faint, but as bitter as her expression. "Who do you think has been accusing me of all manner of sins?'' She tugged her bodice into place, pulled the laces snug and knotted them, her movements abrupt, jerky. '''Twas that old besom!''

Evidently Mary felt safe here, for her voice rose a bit louder with every word. She sat up straight on the bench, no longer seeming to fold in upon herself the way she had outside. Even dirty and tattered as she was, she wore a mantle of self-assurance at odds with her position in the world.

That confidence caught Julianna's notice; intrigued, she observed the woman more closely. Mary might be dressed in a servant's coarse woolen garb, but her bearing could have been learned from Lady Marian herself, had Mary been at Tuck's Tower when Julianna's mother yet lived. By the Virgin, Mary's hands, resting at ease in her lap, were better groomed than her own.

The incongruity jarred loose something that had nagged at the edge of Julianna's awareness in the past; the maid's speech placed her outside a servant's status as well. Though *plain*-spoken, Mary also could sound *well*-spoken, though that seemed to come and go. When they'd been outside, Mary's language had sounded pretty much the same as the other servants'. Just now—in her agitation, perhaps?—she'd reverted to a more refined accent.

"Aye, Mary, you're right, Dora says any number of things, many of them not quite right," Julianna agreed. "Some aren't true at all."

No matter how fervently she might wish for them to be—that they *could* be true.

Restless, she slipped her dagger from her boot, rose and went to stand by the window. Though her attention remained on the room's inhabitants, she absently shifted the knife from hand to hand. "What you heard, Trudy, is completely wrong," she reaffirmed.

Who was she trying to convince? The others, or herself?

Suddenly realizing that her movements bespoke her inner agitation as clearly as her words, she tucked the dagger into her belt and willed her hands to stay motionless, her face to remain calm. "Whatever gossip Dora is spreading doesn't concern me at the moment, however."

A lie, she chided herself. Another sin to do penance for.

The others didn't appear convinced, but any

further protests on her part would only convince them Dora's words were true.

"I brought you all here so we could put an end to the nonsense I saw outside," Julianna added. She rubbed the back of her neck, the movement slow, tired—and the only concession of the bone-deep weariness she felt that she'd permit herself to show. "All you seem to do is to shout and accuse. That serves no useful purpose whatsoever."

Diccon appeared ready to burst out with something, so Julianna nodded for him to speak.

He stood and nodded respectfully to Julianna. "Joan's got things all wrong," he assured her. "Mary's not anything like Joan says."

"Aye," Trudy said tartly. "Joan wouldn't know the truth if it bit her in the arse—I mean backside, beggin' your pardon, milady. But Joan—she's always stirrin' up trouble 'bout somethin'."

Julianna couldn't mistake their sincerity, and she knew herself that gossip ran through the household like wildfire over the slightest thing. Joan tried to defend herself, but Julianna raised her hand to silence her.

The appearance of a beautiful woman like

Mary provided the rumormongers, including Joan and Dora, with a wealth of fodder by her mere existence.

Shame brought a flush to Julianna's cheeks. Had she been as guilty as the others in assuming Mary to be little better than a whore?

She needed to speak with Mary, a conversation better conducted without the others present. "Trudy, Diccon, I'm certain Mary appreciates your defense. I'm glad you were able to keep the mob from harming her further."

Mary nodded, her expression as open as Julianna had ever seen it. "Aye, 'twas kind of you. Otherwise they'd have stoned me for certain."

Julianna crossed the chamber to the door and swung it wide. "You all may go about your business now, with my thanks," she said.

Apparently Trudy and Diccon believed Mary would be safe with her, for they filed past her and left, their expressions untroubled. Joan followed them out of the chamber.

Julianna stood in the doorway and waited, watching until they were all on the other side of the empty great hall before closing the door with a decisive snap.

She turned and leaned back against the door,

arms folded across her chest, her relaxed posture inviting, open.

And completely misleading.

''Now that they've gone, Mary, why don't you tell me who you *really* are, and why you came to Tuck's Tower?''

Chapter Fourteen

William waited deep in the shadows on the landing outside his sickroom, his back pressed against the smooth plaster wall as he listened and looked around to get his bearings. The torches set at intervals along both sides of the hall were unlit, but a faint beam of afternoon sunlight streamed through a window slit high up in the wall at the end of the landing.

He could see well enough, but should be able to remain out of sight as long as he stayed quiet and stayed out of the middle of the hallway.

'Twas his good fortune that Lady Julianna had left so quickly she'd not bothered to call for a guard to watch over him. He wasn't certain how long he'd been unguarded, though since she'd evidently remained by his side during his fever, she'd likely not bothered with one for several days. However long it had been, he was grateful no one had been there now. He felt well enough, considering the circumstances, but he didn't trust his strength to last for long—certainly not long enough to overcome anyone with fighting ability or weapons.

He knew nothing about Tuck's Tower beyond the small storeroom where he'd remained the past few days, save for the view of the courtyard and part of the curtain wall he'd seen from his window. He did know, however, that Lady Julianna's chamber stood behind the large door down the hallway.

Not much information to help him get what he needed and be on his way, but he'd manage fine, just as he usually did.

Since all was quiet below, Will crept to Julianna's door and eased it open. 'Twas very considerate of her to keep her doors so well-oiled, he thought, suppressing a chuckle. As with the storeroom, no squeak or squeal of rusty iron sounded to expose his activities.

'Twas a shame he was stealing into her chamber because she *wasn't* there. In the past, he'd only sought out a woman's room because she would be there waiting for him to join her.

Although in this instance, he was glad she was gone, he told himself.

Aye, and if he believed that fantastical tale, he was just as apt to believe that once he got to Lincoln, the king's regent would gift him with a vast estate for his service to the crown, he thought mockingly.

He might tell himself he was glad to leave Lady Julianna's sphere, but that didn't make it true.

And he'd never been one to lie to himself. The honest truth was that duty and inclination were at war within him, and while he was determined that duty would win the day, it didn't mean he was happy about it.

Find something to jest about in the situation, he told himself. 'Twas his usual way to get through the times when things weren't going the way he wanted, or life grew dangerous.

Humor had often been Will's refuge in life, helping him to see the contrariness of life and fate as he slowly battled his way from yeoman archer's son to a knight in his lord's service. In fact, he was known for his ready wit, and the pranks he carried out on those of high and low degree.

The people he cared about.

He should have been filled with a sense of adventure, of exhilaration. He was on an important mission for Lord Rannulf; he'd escaped the attack in Sherwood Forest with his life, thanks to Lady Julianna and her men; he'd survived his injuries and was on the mend, again thanks to her; he'd spent time alone with a lovely and desirable lady, had held her in his arms, tasted innocence and need in her kisses.

In the past, he'd have been thankful, glad to be given so much.

Now all he could think of was how much more he wanted.

"Ungrateful wretch," Will muttered. Had bettering his station in life made him like a spoiled child, ever greedy for more?

Nay, 'twas simply that he wanted what he knew he could not have.

'Twas the way of life; he knew it, and he knew he could naught but accept it.

He'd stood outlined in the doorway too long, he realized—'twas a wonder he hadn't been caught skulking around. His attention refocused, Will pulled the door closed and crept into the room.

The shutters stood open, the afternoon light casting a pleasant glow over the chamber. While 'twas obvious from the furnishings that a woman lived here, it held little of the sense of luxury he'd noted in the other women's bed chambers he'd seen.

Since Julianna wasn't like other women, he supposed he shouldn't have been surprised by that fact.

The air smelled of her scent, the faint perfume enveloping him in its soft and sensual embrace. His pulse beat faster and his body began to heat from the recollection of Julianna in his arms, warm and soft and delightful. What need had Julianna for fussy linens and tapestries to point out her femininity? The mere fragrance of her hair and skin were a siren's call, sensuous and alluring.

Will shook his head, but he couldn't rid himself of thoughts of Julianna so easily. He needed to get what he came here for, and leave before he got caught.

It took all his willpower, but he forced himself

to concentrate. For if he didn't leave soon, he feared he'd lose the resolve to do so.

'Twas a shame he couldn't hold his breath until he finished searching, he thought with a wry smile. Crossing to the window, he nudged the shutters open for a bit more light and began his search.

Julianna watched Mary carefully as she spoke. The woman remained seated on the bench, not betraying by movement or expression that Julianna's question disturbed her in any way. "I don't understand, milady." She sounded mildly curious, nothing more.

"I believe you understand me just fine, Mary. I wonder, is that truly your name?" Julianna kept her own voice calm, her body at ease against the door. "I'm surprised Joan didn't take you to task for sullying the name of the Virgin," she added dryly. "Though given the sins she accuses you of, perhaps she thinks of you more like Mary Magdalene."

"I'm no more of a sinner than I'm a saint," Mary replied. The heat of anger simmered in her dark eyes and resonated in her words, her only reaction.

"That's not what Joan and the others said," Julianna reminded her. "They want to cast you from the gates, far from their men so you won't tempt them." She unfolded her arms, straightened from the door and began to pace the confines of the small room. "Other than Rolf—who I know is loyal to his wife and thus immune to your wiles—I can't imagine any of the other men-at-arms would appeal much to a beautiful woman such as you. If whoring was in truth your aim, you'd have done better in Nottingham." She paused by the window. "Or Lincoln, perhaps. The king's army is there, plenty of opportunity for an enterprising woman," she pointed out.

Please take the bait, she begged silently. *Do something—anything—so I can cease to taunt and torment you!*

Mary gazed down at her hands, her cheeks pale, but still she remained silent.

Julianna forced herself to stay where she was, when she could gladly have grabbed Mary and shaken her. Julianna was convinced she was right, that Mary was no whore. What would it take to make her fight back?

"Why did you come to Tuck's Tower?" Julianna asked. "'Tis a pleasant place, of course, though I admit my partiality, since I've lived here all my life. But I cannot imagine why it would appeal to a stranger. We have little commerce with the outside world, nor are we so comfortable that any of us can afford the luxury of idleness.'' She reached for the pitcher of ale on the table and poured herself a cup, pausing to drink it down and not bothering to offer any to Mary.

The woman must be thirsty, considering her dusty state. However, if she were indeed a servant, she'd not expect her mistress to offer her anything.

Mary glanced away as Julianna poured ale into another cup. ''Did you come here thinking to earn coin for your labors? If that was your aim—whether your profession be that of healer or something else—you most surely chose the wrong place. You must be sorely disappointed.''

Tired and out of patience, with both Mary and herself, Julianna pushed the cup across the table toward the other woman. ''Here. You must be parched,'' she said, not bothering any longer to imbue her voice with the nasty tone she'd used earlier.

Mary didn't reach for it, but she looked up and met Julianna's gaze, then slowly rose to her feet.

"Rachel." She curtsied. "My name is Rachel Belleville, Lady Julianna. I ask that you give me sanctuary."

Will leaned on the edge of the trunk at the foot of the bed and carefully dug through the contents in his search for his message pouch. Weapons and armor he found aplenty, but little else. Of course, considering there was no way to lock the trunk, he should have expected he'd find nothing of importance there.

Except for a way to arm himself.

God curse him for a fool! Tossing caution to the wind, he searched the contents of the trunk until he found a well-used dagger of a size and shape similar to his own—not his, but near enough. He'd discovered no sign of his armor or weapons in Julianna's chamber, unfortunately. No doubt they'd been put away where he'd never find them. Though he'd prefer his own, he could manage with just about anything. 'Twas only in recent years that he'd had the benefit of decent weapons of his own choosing.

He did wish he had his own dagger, however, but no doubt that blade still resided snug in Julianna's boot top.

He'd always believed the dagger to be a talisman of good fortune; now it had the good fortune to rest against Julianna's leg.

By Christ's bones, had he suddenly become a maudlin idiot? He'd be wishing she carried the blade tucked in the neckline of her shirt next!

Mayhap he truly had lost his wits. It hadn't even occurred to him to try to regain the weapon earlier, when they'd been standing wound around each other in the next room. If she'd been as distracted as he had, she most likely wouldn't have noticed him steal back the dagger.

He gave a mirthless laugh; he'd been in no condition, mentally or physically, to wrest control of much of anything from Julianna at that point. If he were honest with himself, she could have done anything she wanted with him then, and he wouldn't have put up much of a struggle.

Will closed the trunk and turned away from the bed. That piece of furniture gave him too many ideas, none of them wise or likely to happen, either. He'd looked through nearly every hiding place in the chamber already; he couldn't see anyplace else to look.

Although that might be the ruse—the hiding

place wasn't obvious. Will slowly turned and scanned the room once more.

A section of the hearth caught his attention, for the stone edge didn't appear quite even. Grinning, he knelt before the fireplace and wedged the slim dagger blade between the stones. The weapon slid in neatly, and the top stone popped loose, revealing a dark hole wider than his fist.

Will set the rock aside and plunged his hand into the opening. 'Twas deep—his arm was in it nearly to his elbow. His fingers brushed against something that felt like parchment; he sighed with relief and, closing his hand around the cylinder, slid it from the hole.

"Damnation!" Disappointment swept through him as soon as he saw the roll of parchment scrolls. They were too old and yellowed with age to be the messages he'd carried.

Curiosity wouldn't permit him to return the documents to their hiding place unseen, however. He'd always been too inquisitive for his own good, his father had told him that often enough. Will sat back on his haunches and turned toward the window so he could see the faded writing more clearly.

What he read amazed him, made his childhood memories rush to the forefront of his thoughts.

If what he read here was true, 'twas beyond anything he'd ever imagined then or since. Maid Marian and Robin of the Hood had been real people.

And Julianna d'Arcy was their daughter.

Chapter Fifteen

"Rachel Belleville?" Julianna didn't bother to try to hide her astonishment. "What relation are you to Richard?" she demanded. "You *are* related to him, I assume."

Rachel nodded, her expression unhappy. "He is my brother."

Cursing beneath her breath, Julianna took a turn about the chamber, its narrow confines no salve to her need to pace away her agitation. Dear Lord in heaven, how had this come about? Her avaricious neighbor's sister here in her own keep—living as a servant or worse, if Joan were to be believed....

"Does he know you're here?" Julianna asked, then pounded her fist on the table in frustration. "Of course he does! He must know—he's always poking his nose into my business, how could he not—"

"Milady." Rachel cut short Julianna's tirade. "Richard has no idea I'm here. He believes I've gone south, to stay with our sister and her husband on their farm."

Julianna glanced at the other woman, somewhat reassured by Rachel's apparent sincerity. "Then what are you doing here?" she demanded.

A stubborn expression settled onto Rachel's face. "Must I tell you?"

"I insist," Julianna told her crisply. "Surely you don't expect me to give sanctuary, as you put it, to my enemy's sister without knowing why." She poured herself more ale and held the cool pewter mug against her temple. She suddenly felt overwhelmed by exhaustion, the tension of dealing with Will, and now this. Any more trouble, and her pulse might burst through her aching head at that specific point. "I'm waiting."

Rachel sat down on the bench and twisted her hands into the soiled fabric of her skirt. "I came to stay with my brother last fall. I didn't mind Richard's temper too much—as long as I stayed out of his way, we got along fine. And 'twas far better than living with our sister, for she married beneath her, so Richard says, and they really didn't have any place for me. I like Birkland, and kept busy caring for the sick and injured, much as I've done here.''

"I doubt Richard made you sleep in the barracks with his men," Julianna pointed out.

"He wouldn't permit me near them."

Julianna sat down at the table and, leaning her elbows on the smooth oak, rested her head on her hands. "I cannot wait to learn what he plans for me since you've spent most of your stay here with my men." Her pulse thundered louder at the thought. "You were telling me how you came to be here, were you not?" She glanced up and gave Rachel an impatient look. "Just tell me, would you please?"

Rachel stood and approached Julianna. "I fell in love with someone Richard considered unsuitable—one of his knights—so he sent me away." She reached down and gently eased the tousled hair away from Julianna's face. "I refused to travel so far from my beloved, so I tried to remain nearby. I thought if I could hide here, perhaps we could leave the area together someday soon."

Rachel's hands stroked soothingly over Julianna's aching brow. "You do know I'm a healer?" she asked.

Julianna closed her eyes for a moment, then opened them to find the other woman watching her. "I've heard any number of things about you, Rachel, too many of them to all be true. Until a little while ago I believed you to be a drink-loving, man-stealing whore—none of which is actually true, I imagine." She straightened and, though it pained her to do so, shrugged away Rachel's relaxing touch. "I wish I'd realized that sooner, for I would have insisted you care for Will Bowman. You would have been far better than I at stitching him up."

Rachel's laugh surprised Julianna. "But if you hadn't had a chance to care for him yourself, how could you have fallen in love with him?" she teased.

Julianna tried to glare at Rachel, but the movement hurt too much. "Trudy didn't know what she was talking about," she said, her voice fading as her stomach began to churn. Groaning, she laid her head on the table and closed her eyes.

"Lady Julianna!" Rachel swept aside her hair and laid a hand on Julianna's cheek.

"Sick," Julianna mumbled. "Need bed."

"I'll get someone to help," Rachel told her.

"No." She braced her hands on the table and levered herself to her feet. Though she felt like her head would roll off her shoulders, through sheer force of will she ignored the pain and pushed away from the table. She'd felt this way before, and knew 'twould only get worse. Thus far, however, she'd kept these bouts of sickness a secret. "Don't want them to know."

"You cannot mean to go upstairs without help," Rachel protested. "I could get Diccon, or Rolf—"

"No. If you help me across the hall and up the stairs, I'll manage."

Feet scuffing unsteadily through the rushes scattered across the floor, with Rachel's assistance Julianna made her way to her chamber. Once they'd climbed the stairs, Julianna sent the other woman away, refusing her offer of a draught or company. She needed a dark room and silence more than anything else.

She unlatched the door. It swung open easily, and she stumbled through the portal, nearly tripping over Will as he levered himself up off the floor.

He caught hold of her and steadied her on her feet.

"What are you doing?" she demanded in a weak voice. She tried to pull away from him, but her head spun and she swayed into him.

"What's wrong?" Will caught her about the waist and held her upright. "Are you ill?"

She shook her head, an action she regretted at once. "No. Just tired."

His blue eyes full of concern, he scanned her face. "You *are* ill! Let me help you onto the bed, then I'll get one of the women to take care of you."

Julianna caught his arm and stopped him before he could try to pick her up. "Don't!" Jesu, was he as foolish as she? If he managed to get her off her feet, they'd both end up flat on the floor. "I can walk. Just help me to the bed."

She had to close her eyes to block the sharp light streaming into the room, but she made it across the room with Will's assistance. The soft mattress was an island of calm in a turbulent sea; she sprawled facedown upon it with a sigh of relief.

"Should I call for Dora, or one of the other women?" Will asked. He sat beside her and smoothed her hair out of the way, the stroke of his hand a balm to ease away her pain.

"No, no one," she whispered. "I don't want them to know."

"Not know that you're ill? I would assume that even the mighty Lady Julianna d'Arcy is permitted to rest, or to take the time to recover when she's ill."

She reached for his hand where it rested beside hers on the bed. "You don't understand." She paused to collect her thoughts. Did she dare reveal to a stranger—for Will *was* a stranger to her—the facts she'd not admitted to anyone else at Tuck's Tower? "'Tis a secret, one I'd rather not tell anyone here."

"If you're willing to let me leave, I'll not be here much longer myself, Julianna. I have things I must do, duties I've already delayed too long." He raised her hand to his lips and pressed a kiss into her palm, then closed her fingers over it. "But if you'll trust me with your secrets, I vow I'll not reveal them to another soul. And if you need my help, I promise that once I've fulfilled my obligation to my overlord, I will return to Tuck's Tower and assist you in any way I can."

She could feel her remaining strength fading.

What should she do? 'Twas so difficult to decide, to know who to trust…. Though she and Will hadn't spoken of it, she knew in her heart that he was no ally of Richard Belleville's. Nor did he seem to find anything strange about a noble-woman ruling a keep.

If she must confide in a man, ask his help, she didn't know of anyone else to confide in.

Starting with her current malady.

Will could see the play of conflicting emotions in Julianna's wan face. In truth, he didn't know how she was able to converse at all. Though her voice sounded slurred and her speech was slow, still she struggled to make him understand.

He didn't know why she was so determined to hide her illness from her own servants, but she was not one to do anything without a reason. He'd help her in any way he could.

He bent to place a kiss on her brow. "Will you trust me, milady? I vow I'll never betray you."

Her hand firm in his, Julianna nodded. "Thank you, Sir William," she said formally, her tone and their words bringing to mind an oath of fealty.

"Thank you for your confidence," he whispered.

Before he could say more, Julianna's eyes rolled back and her hand went limp in his grasp.

Dear God, he'd just promised he'd not tell anyone about this.

Now what should he do?

Chapter Sixteen

Birkland

Sir Richard took a last look at the square of parchment in his hand before crumpling the letter and tossing it in the fire. Damned fools! Always putting their plots and plans in writing, where they might come back to haunt them later.

He'd have kept the missives himself, as possible protection in the future, if not for the fact that the messages contained too much that could incriminate him, as well.

He leaned on the mantle and watched the parchment turn to ash. Damnation! He slammed his fist against the wooden slab, barely feeling the pain of the blow.

Everything seemed to be crumbling away. Their plans to overthrow young King Henry and put their own man in place as their new monarch were not going well. Old Lord William, the Earl of Pembroke, had lost none of his wiliness with age, unfortunately. The old bastard had foiled their scheme to move several men into the king's household, ruining their best plot.

They weren't fools; they'd hoped to dispose of King John's whelp without anyone the wiser that the lad had been helped from this life to the next. Nice and tidy, without the time and expense of mounting a siege, as was currently under way at Lincoln. Nor did it involve entrusting too many with the details of their strategy.

Richard pressed his now-aching fist to his lips as he considered what his own next step should be. He hadn't heard anything more for several days from the fools he'd sent out after Bowman, and the last message simply said that they'd discovered no trace of him. Nigh a week had passed since they'd escorted Lord Rannulf's messenger on his way; if not for the fact that Richard had Bowman's horse in his stable, 'twas as though the man had completely disappeared once he left Birkland.

That might serve his purpose just as well as if they'd found him, save that 'twould have been a great benefit to gain possession of the sack of messages Bowman had carried. Richard knew the man had been headed to Lincoln next, no doubt carrying information for Pembroke, the king's regent.

Information no doubt of great use to Richard and his own plans.

Still, with Bowman gone—dead, most likely— he shouldn't have to worry about Lord Rannulf removing Birkland from his control or ruining his plans.

There was naught else he could do about any of that now, however, but to wait. Instead he would be better served to think of other options, new ways to advance his own position in life.

'Twould have to be a woman, unfortunately.

Which one? he wondered. Should he re-establish his campaign to gain Tuck's Tower for himself? He had two choices there: wed Lady Julianna, or take the castle from her by force. Neither plan appealed to him much. He'd rather not attempt to marry that she-devil—assuming he could get close enough to her to do so. Given her reputed skill at arms, he'd likely become her *dead* husband before the ink had dried on their marriage contract.

As for taking Tuck's Tower by force...Lady Julianna's troops might not be great in number, but they were well-trained, far better skilled than his own, he feared. Rumor had it that there were still remnants of Robin of the Hood's legendary Merry Men lurking somewhere in the vicinity as well, ready to take up her cause for her parents' sakes.

Assuming, of course, that any of them were still alive, they must be ancient by now—but 'twas a possibility he should consider. He preferred to plan well for all his schemes; he'd found they tended to work out better that way.

If he chose not to try for Tuck's Tower—though the place was a temptation, he must admit—he could always send for his sister Rachel to return, and find her a good husband to marry.

A man Richard could control, and preferably one with plenty of lands and money he was willing to share. No yeoman farmer for Rachel! She was a beauty, far better marriage barter than their older sister had been.

Rachel should have learned her lesson by now, no doubt, after several months spent swilling pigs and caring for their numerous nieces and nephews. She knew better than to disobey him now. All he needed to do was to find a good prospect to wed her, and he'd be set.

'Twas a better plan by far than dealing with Lady Julianna, though he wouldn't toss that scheme aside just yet, either. Perhaps if he were to find a way to be rid of her, her people would surely be upset, in disarray...he would be able to take command while chaos reigned, with no one the wiser that he'd been behind Lady Julianna's death or disappearance.

It might work....

He poured wine into a goblet and swirled the liquid, staring into its crimson depths as he considered what to do. The drink reminded him of blood and battle—two of his least favorite things.

He'd send for Rachel, he decided. She'd never dare refuse him, and she'd serve his purpose well. 'Twould be the safest course to assure himself of gaining everthing he desired.

As for his plot against the king...

Was it truly worth the risk?

Though he was beginning to doubt it was the best way to make his fortune, only time could provide the answer to that.

* * *

Tuck's Tower

Completely unsure what to do, Will stared down at Julianna. She was still breathing, but she didn't respond when he called her name.

Should he move her? Try to prop her up?

He wasn't certain what had happened, what was wrong with her. It appeared she'd swooned, although she'd seemed ill, groggy beforehand.

He pressed his palm to her cheek. No fever, but her face looked pale. Even her lips had lost their reddish tinge, and a small spattering of pale freckles he'd not noticed before was visible along her cheekbones.

By Christ's bones, why had he made that promise to her? Surely Dora would know what to do.

But he'd sworn to Julianna; he'd not break that vow unless it appeared her life was in danger.

Someone rapped on the door leading from the chamber next door. Will stood and crossed to answer it, glad of the chance to at least ask someone for help.

He opened the door and discovered a rather disheveled maidservant standing there, a large basket filled with small bundles and bunches of dried plants propped on one hip.

"Is Lady Julianna all right?" she asked.

Will blocked her view of the room with his body, but the impertinent wench stood on tiptoe and tried to look past him. "I'm sure she is."

He tried to close the door, but she thrust herself into the gap before he could swing the heavy portal closed. "What are you about?" he asked, still keeping her out of Julianna's chamber.

"She was unwell when I helped her up the stairs earlier. I'm a healer," she told him. She held up the basket. "I thought mayhap I could help her."

If she already knew Julianna was ill, there was no reason why he should keep her from her mistress. Clearly Julianna hadn't realized that her malady—whatever it might be—was not as secret as she believed.

"Come in." He let her into the room, then closed the door quickly, lest anyone else who was in the other chamber look in.

The maid gave him a strange look, but ignored him as soon as she saw Julianna on the bed. "What happened?" she asked as she hurried to her mistress's side.

"She collapsed nigh as soon as she got here," he told her.

"I knew I shouldn't have left her!" Setting the basket on the bed, she began to examine Julianna. "Was she able to speak?"

"Aye, though not clearly. I could tell something was wrong, but she wouldn't allow me to get help," he explained. "It looked as if she swooned just before you knocked."

She nodded absently. "Bring me the water pitcher," she ordered, her attention focused on her patient. "And the basin as well."

Though surprised to be ordered about by the young woman, Will did as she asked.

In no time the maid had settled Julianna in the bed, closing the bed curtains and undressing her without Will's help after she'd shooed him out of her way and sent him to wait near the hearth.

He took up a thick stick from the pile of kindling on the hearthstones and carved away at it while he waited. 'Twas little more than a toothpick by the time the servant finally turned away from the bed and began to pack her herbs in the basket.

"Is she all right?" He left his post and crossed to stand at the foot of the bed.

He could see Julianna through a slit in the curtains. She lay propped on the pillows, the bedding tucked beneath her arms, her shoulders bare save for a golden medallion she wore around her neck. She looked so serene and still, 'twas difficult for him to believe it was Julianna lying there.

"She will be fine once she's slept, I believe." She wiped her hands on a length of linen and joined him by the bed. "'Tis a headache."

"A headache! She looked nigh dead! How can that be?" he asked.

"'Tis an ailment not many suffer, thank the Virgin. Very painful, with little to be done for it. If I had some poppy juice, 'twould help her sleep, but the tisane I gave her should work well enough." She sighed. "I should have realized once I heard her speak—she could scarce form the words."

"I thank you for your care of her," Will said, his gratitude heartfelt. "I had no notion how to help her. What should I do now?"

"Let her rest, milord. 'Tis all the medicine she needs."

"I'm no lord," he protested.

"But you are a knight, aren't you? Should I call you 'sir' then?"

"Call me whatever you like, it matters not to me," he said, impatient to return to Julianna's side. Though he could do little, at least he could remain with her in case she needed him. She'd done the same for him, after all.

Besides, he needed to stay with her. The sight of her sprawled across the bed, apparently lifeless, had jolted him, made him realize that despite his earlier plan to simply leave Tuck's Tower—to leave Julianna—he could not. Though her ailment provided him the perfect opportunity to slip away unhindered, he refused to take that cowardly course.

He rounded the bed and sat on the edge of the mattress, careful not to jostle Julianna. To his worried gaze her color seemed more normal, though she barely moved except to moan quietly every so often.

After a while he realized that the maid had remained as well. She'd taken a seat on the edge of the hearth, sorting through her herbs.

"You need not stay," he told her. "I'll send for you once she awakens." He didn't know her name, however. "Who shall I ask for?"

She stood and curtsied, the courtesy more formal than he'd expected. Now that he thought of it, her speech was finer than usual for a servant.

"My name is Rachel Belleville, Sir William. Richard Belleville is my brother."

Belleville! Will glanced from Julianna to Rachel, from Rachel to the piles of herbs scattered across the hearth.

She'd been with Julianna earlier, before she'd collapsed. Eyes narrowing, Will stood and crossed the chamber in three long strides.

Rachel stood there unmoving, even when he grabbed her by the shoulders and shook her. "What have you done to Julianna?" he demanded, his voice harsh. He shook her again. "Did your brother send you here to harm her?"

Chapter Seventeen

Julianna awoke to the sound of voices, low-pitched but angry nonetheless. She carefully opened her eyes—the dim light of dusk filtered into the chamber, soft enough that she could bear to keep her eyes open.

By shifting her head on the pillow, she could see Will and Rachel standing near the hearth, arguing.

She raised herself up and crawled over the mattress toward the foot of the bed. "What is going on?" she demanded.

Though her voice sounded weak as a mewling kitten, the combatants heard her and ceased their squabbling.

Suddenly realizing she was naked, she eased herself down on the coverlet and tugged at the sheet until she could wrap it about herself. Though all she wanted to do at the moment was to slump down and close her eyes, she forced herself to prop herself up on her elbow and peer at them over the footboard.

"Julianna!" Will spun about and headed for her, pushing aside the bed curtains and reaching for her. He gathered her up into his arms and held her to him as though she were precious.

She grabbed at her makeshift garb, gathering the linen in one hand and resting against Will's chest, for she couldn't let pass the chance to be in his arms.

'Twas a wonderful sensation, precisely what she needed at the moment, for the headache had left her feeling frail and fragile.

And quite disgusted by her body's betrayal. She had no time to give in to illness—nor did she enjoy the pain of it.

"Milady, you shouldn't be moving about," Rachel chided, standing back respectfully until Will eased his grip and lowered Julianna down onto the bed.

Julianna peered up at Rachel, her thoughts growing more clear by the instant. "What are you doing here?" she asked.

"Do you know who she is?" Will demanded, interrupting Rachel's attempt to speak.

"Aye, I do," Julianna told him. *By the Virgin, she hadn't the energy to deal with this now!* "And I trust her. After all, I know at least as much about her as I do of *you*." She shifted so she could see them better. "I told Rachel earlier to leave me. I was surprised to see her here, 'tis all."

Neither Rachel nor Will appeared comfortable, with each other or her. Were they both feeling guilty? As well they ought, she thought darkly, since neither should be here. Hadn't she told them both to leave her be?

A dull ache still pounded behind her eyes, making her bad-tempered and impatient. If she were wise, she'd send them both on their way and go back to sleep, lest she cause more trouble for herself with ill-considered words.

But just then her memory of Will's promise returned full force, infuriating her more. He hadn't merely said he'd protect her secrets, he'd sworn to do so. "Does your word mean so little, Sir William?"

He met her angry gaze with a glare of his own. "How could you believe I would break my oath to you?" he inquired stiffly, his blue eyes pale and cold. "Rachel came here to help you, and she appeared to know how to do so. I didn't. Should I have turned her away, when you so obviously needed her?"

His words made her feel lower than a worm. She, who had been schooled in knightly ways, certainly knew better than to question a man's sense of honor.

"I beg your pardon, Will." She reached out to him; hesitating but a moment, he caught her hand in his. "I'm too quick-tempered and easily riled. I shouldn't have doubted you."

He raised her hand to his lips. "You're forgiven." His eyes warmed as he looked down at her.

Julianna followed his gaze and saw why. She jerked the sheet—which scarcely clung to her breasts—up around her throat. "I believe you should leave so I can dress," she informed him. "Though I don't suggest you go far. Now that we're both feeling better, I believe 'tis past time we discussed why you're here, who you're associated with—" her head still felt as though 'twould crack at the slightest provocation, but she wriggled off the edge of the high mattress to stand beside the bed ''—and what you were doing with my private documents.''

Will's questioning look was unconvincing.

Julianna held on to the bedpost and tried to convey a sense of command and strength. ''You needn't deny it, for I did see you with them. And I *will* have an explanation—soon.''

Unsurprised by Julianna's sudden suspicion, Will took his leave of her and returned to the chamber beside hers. In his absence the place had been cleaned: the pallet was neatly pushed against the wall; soap, a basin of fresh water, and clean clothing awaited his pleasure. Sighing his gratitude, he rubbed his whisker-covered chin and took up a candle and flint to light the room more.

He hadn't been certain Julianna had noticed the roll of parchment he'd held when she entered her room earlier, for it had been obvious she could barely function. He had questions for Julianna as well, questions about Rachel Belleville, and why she was here at Tuck's Tower.

'Twas just as well they were to talk soon, for talk was a commodity that had been in short supply during their brief association.

In spite of that, he felt he knew Julianna well,

that the way he felt about her wasn't a simple matter of his cock ruling his head. He wanted her, aye—what man with blood in his veins wouldn't?—but he also enjoyed her company and her lively ways.

Since he hadn't been able to make his escape from Tuck's Tower and its mistress, he might as well take that fact as a sign that he should use any time they spent together as an opportunity to know her better. If she'd give him back his message pouch, he'd happily deliver the missives, then return here on his way back to Lord Rannulf's.

He'd realized, when he sat watching over Julianna as she slept, that he wanted to build some sort of relationship with her. If friendship was her aim, he thought he could make do with that, though he knew he'd rather have more from her.

Preferably her body, he thought with a wry laugh—that and more.

A frightening thought, but one he believed was inevitable.

One that didn't frighten him nearly as much as the concept of *not* seeing her again.

He felt surprisingly well, mind and body, especially considering he'd been senseless with fever a day earlier.

Perhaps his life was about to take a turn for the better!

His mood light, Will stripped and set about making himself presentable. If he wanted more from Julianna, he'd better make the best use of every advantage.

What would she think of him once he was clean, shaved and capable of remaining on his feet for longer than a moment?

Julianna leaned against the bedpost as soon as the door to the storeroom closed behind Will. "I thank you for your care of me, Rachel," she said. "I doubt I'd yet be able to lift my head without it."

Rachel hurried to Julianna's side and, taking hold of her arm, assisted her as she climbed back onto the edge of the bed. She sat down beside Julianna and arranged the covers about her. "I wish you'd have let me stay to help you before, for perhaps 'twould have eased your pain the sooner."

Julianna, struggling up out of the cocoon of sheets and blankets, gave a rueful chuckle. "True.

But then I wouldn't have had the pleasure of waking with Will beside me in my bed."

"Lady Julianna!" A tide of pink swept up over Rachel's cheeks.

"No matter how closely Diccon and the other men watched over you, after the amount of time you've spent in the barracks, I cannot believe you'd be embarrassed by what I just said," Julianna said as she propped herself up against the mound of pillows.

"'Tisn't what you said—'tis that *you* said it," Rachel informed her. "Unless I misunderstood you?"

"Nay, you took my meaning clear enough." For some reason Julianna felt comfortable with Rachel in a way she hadn't felt with other women, able to speak her mind. Though she didn't know why that should be so, she had no intention of ignoring so rare a connection. "What woman wouldn't be best pleased to awaken with Will Bowman by her side?" she added teasingly.

Rachel's gaze rested upon Julianna's face for a moment, as if measuring her state of mind. Then, amusement brightening her eyes, she shook her head. "Not I. I've never been partial to blond, blue-eyed, handsome men. If his hair were dark, however...."

"I'm sure we could ask Sir Will if he has any friends or compatriots—a brother, mayhap?—who would meet your requirements," Julianna informed her, trying unsuccessfully to keep her expression serious.

She burst out laughing at once, Rachel joining in.

Her head still hurt, though not so badly. Shared merriment appeared to be a powerful medicine. A glance at Rachel, as the other woman continued to smile, lightened her own mood greatly. "Shall I ask him?" Julianna inquired, only half joking.

The amusement faded from Rachel's eyes. "'Twould serve no purpose. My brother would never permit me to wed where he had not chosen."

Julianna remembered the reason Rachel had fled to Tuck's Tower and felt a fool. "I'm sorry, Rachel. I forgot that you'd a sweetheart already."

"Do you know, I've scarce thought of Roger since I left Birkland," Rachel said. "I've wondered if perhaps he was so appealing to me simply because I knew Richard wouldn't approve of him."

"Because he was forbidden to you?"

"Nay—because I knew deep inside that, no matter what I'd done with Roger, I'd never be allowed to remain with him. 'Twas safe to—" Rachel glanced away "—experiment with him. I know now that Roger never touched my emotions."

Curious, Julianna watched Rachel closely. "How do you know that? How can you tell?"

Rachel shrugged and turned to face her. "I realize now that 'twas the idea of kissing a man that made my heart beat faster, not the fact that Roger was the man I was kissing."

"Do you mean that *any* man would have made you feel the same?" Julianna couldn't imagine such a thing! 'Twas Will she wanted to kiss—and more.

No one else would do.

"Not quite *any* man, but an attractive man who appealed to me." She nodded. "Aye, I believe 'twould have had the same effect."

Julianna mulled that over for but a moment. As astounding as she found the fact, she knew she'd never wanted any man the way she'd wanted Will Bowman—since the moment she'd held him, had seen his face, reveled in his scent.

To her, Will embodied all that was male.

She'd not felt that sensation of *rightness* before, and she doubted she'd feel it with anyone else.

Rachel reached over and gave Julianna's hand a brief squeeze. "I've little doubt you make Sir Will's heart beat faster. Does he do the same to yours?"

"Is it so obvious?" Julianna's pulse quickened as Rachel's first comment sank into her brain. "Do you really think so?"

"Yes and yes," Rachel said. A smile on her face, she rose. "That being so, what shall we do about it?"

"Do we need to do anything?"

"Do you think the fish bites at an empty hook?" Rachel asked. She crossed the chamber to the chest below the window and raised the lid, sending the fragrant scent of Lady Marian's perfume wafting through the room. "What have you here for bait, milady?"

Curious as to Rachel's intention, Julianna swung her legs over the edge of the bed and stood, winding the sheet around her as a make-shift robe. "I can scarce recall what garb is stored away there," she said as she joined Rachel, bending to peer into the coffer.

She dropped to her knees and carefully lifted out the first garment, a dark green gown of fine silk embroidered around the neckline with pearls and gold thread. "My mother made this for me, though I've never worn it." She laid it in her lap, nearly giving in to the urge to bury her face in the cool material that bore her mother's scent. Every stitch had been made with love, Julianna knew, a gift for the daughter Lady Marian had cherished.

Rachel knelt as well and smoothed her finger reverently over the intricate design. "'Tis lovely." She glanced at Julianna, her eyes lingering on the mass of disheveled hair and the sheet drooping off one shoulder. Her gaze contemplative, she slipped her hands gently beneath the gown and lifted it up against Julianna's face. "The gold and green make your eyes and skin glow," Rachel said. "Your mother knew well what would suit you." She nodded her approval. "Aye, this will do nicely, should you wish to capture Sir Will. He'll not be able to resist you in this."

Rather than giving Julianna confidence, Rachel's certainty brought all Julianna's doubts to the fore. Despite her mother's tutelage, she knew next to nothing about how to dress and act the lady.

If she attempted such a feat, would she simply appear an unfeminine woman, a pathetic figure who had resorted to female wiles to attract a man?

"Come, Lady Julianna." Rachel laid the gown across Julianna's lap and reached into the chest, drawing out an undertunic of soft gold and a while silk chemise so finely woven it reminded Julianna of mist. "You cannot ignore such beautiful clothes. 'Tis the perfect garb to catch Sir Will's eye, though I think you've done that already," she added. "If you feel well enough, I'll help you dress and arrange your hair."

Considering that Rachel had managed to look appealing even when bedaubed with dust and filth—she'd found an opportunity since then to wash and change her gown, Julianna noted—perhaps 'twould be useful to see what Rachel had in mind.

'Twould give her an opportunity to question Rachel further as well, while they were occupied with other pursuits. Since she was feeling less inclination to interrogate the other woman, mayhap a simple conversation between them might be more effective.

More like something friends might do.

Her scruples appeased, Julianna gathered the gown to her chest and rose to her feet. "I'd like that," she told Rachel. "Though whether I'm doing this for Will or for myself, I have no idea."

"It matters not a whit which it is, milady." Taking Julianna by the arm, Rachel led her to a stool by the hearth. Smiling, she added, "'Twill be enjoyable either way, will it not?"

Chapter Eighteen

Julianna stood by the stand of candles Rachel had placed by the window and gaped at her face in the polished steel mirror the other woman held.

Rachel had brought about a miraculous transformation. Julianna stared at her reflection, scarcely able to believe that she was that elegant creature. Rachel's gentle touch had eased Julianna's headache while taming her unruly curls into a coil of neatly twined braids woven with gold ribbons. A sheer veil framed Julianna's face and lent her an air of elegance.

As for the gown...tears welled in Julianna's eyes when she considered how well the green and gold became her. The silk hugged her body, the sensuous slide of the fabric over her skin making her feel every bit a woman. The pearls stitched around the neck of the gown lent a luminous glow to her face.

The flush of pink tinting her cheeks, however, she attributed to her pleasure at her own appearance. "Thank you for the gift, *Maman*," she whispered as she smoothed her hand over the silk once again. How her mother had discerned what would become her, Julianna didn't know, but she was very glad she'd given in to Rachel's suggestion.

She was only sorry she'd waited so long to wear the clothes.

"Ready to bait the hook, Lady Julianna?" Rachel asked with a mischievous look.

"I am indeed." Julianna returned her smile and swept past Rachel to the door. "Would you please have someone tell Sir William that I await him in the garden?" She tugged the door open. "They'll need to show him where I'll be."

Feeling as well-equipped for combat—or something like it, she thought with a grin—as if she were armed with her sword and dagger, Julianna set out for the battlefield she'd chosen.

Victory would be hers.

She'd make certain of it.

* * *

Will trod the winding path through the herb garden with impatient steps. A servant had led him to the narrow entrance, told him to follow the walk, and left him to find his way through the dimly lit foliage.

He brushed up against bushes and leaves, releasing a myriad of scents. The fragrance lingered on the night air and heightened his senses—as if they needed any further stimulation.

The mere thought of Julianna awaiting him was enough to send his wits reeling. He couldn't erase the image of her sprawled on her bed, her glorious body barely concealed by a sheet and her hair spread about her like a silken cloak. Like a fool, he'd thought of little else since he'd left her chamber; the memory had roused his body and clouded his mind. His injuries were nigh forgotten as his rebellious passion clamored for Julianna.

He knew they'd much to discuss; secrets to be revealed, thoughts to be shared…plans to be made, if he had his way.

Though not necessarily in that order, he thought with a quiet laugh.

Will rounded a corner past a tall plant and found Julianna seated on a bench. She rose as he approached, moving more fully into the glow of a torch.

She stole his breath. The feminine garb she wore shimmered in the flickering light, making her appear a mystical creature made up of moon-beams and dreams. Her gown hugged curves his hands recognized but his eyes had not seen. The neat coils of dark hair beneath her veil made his fingers ache to touch, to unwind the complicated plaits and bury his hands in Julianna's soft curls.

She moved, but the image remained unbroken.

Not an illusion, but a woman.

His woman.

Julianna.

"Sir Will, I'm pleased you could join me." Her voice held an unfamiliar note—low, husky and seductive. She sat on the bench again, sliding over to make room for him beside her.

Feeling as though he'd stepped into a dream, Will accepted her unspoken invitation and sat down. The bench was just wide enough for them both, placing them thigh to thigh, shoulder to shoulder. Her warmth seeped into him through the thin fabric of her clothing, heating his blood and honing his senses to a higher pitch.

The fragrance he thought of as Julianna's came

to him even over the perfume of the garden, its sweetness a perfect accompaniment to the heady night scent surrounding them. He took her hand and brought it to his lips. "My lady," he whispered, his gaze meeting hers and holding it captive. "Tell me what you want of me."

For a moment Julianna hesitated, unsure whether her disordered wits were capable of anything more than to demand he kiss her, that they surrender to the seduction of the night and let it take them where it would. She slipped her fingers free of his hold, but that liberty did little to diminish the spell holding them captive.

She shook her head and rose, stepping away from him and nearly falling backward into a bed of lavender. "I cannot think with you so near," she protested. "Damnation, that wasn't what I meant to say!"

Will stood and moved toward her in one smooth motion, trapping her. "Then say nothing," he murmured.

"Stop." She held up her hand, whether to halt his words or to keep him at bay, she had no notion. "Will, we cannot remain here. 'Tis too—"

"—too tempting? Seductive?" He reached up and tugged her veil away from her face, slowly winding the gauzy fabric around his fingers as it slipped off her hair. "Not conducive to reasonable thought?" He leaned close and lightly touched the corner of her mouth with his tongue.

She thought her knees might give way if he didn't cease his torment.

"Julianna, love, you made me feel that way in the storeroom you put me in, with me wearing a blanket and you in men's garb." He pressed a kiss to her cheek, then nuzzled her ear. He'd shaved; the brush of his smooth chin over her skin, and the scent of soap rising from him, made her heart race. "As beautiful as you are, and this place is, it makes little difference. You befuddle my mind and my senses."

She could barely draw a breath.

"We could go up on the wall," she told him, her voice faint. "The wind will clear our minds, and the guards will assure we behave ourselves."

Perhaps—though at the moment, she had her doubts *anything* could keep her passion in check.

Will leaned against her, pressed his cheek to hers and sighed. "As you wish, milady." Before she could respond, he caught her about the waist and swung her around to face the path. "Come along, Julianna," he urged as he pulled her back through the garden. "I promise I'll behave," he said, laughing. "As long as you do."

Catching his enthusiasm, her heart light, she let him tug her along in his wake.

I'll not promise anything, she vowed silently, *for I don't intend to miss a moment of what we might share.*

The wind gusted through the narrow crenels atop the wall, pressing Julianna's gown against her body and tugging her hair loose from the neat braids and coils Rachel had fashioned earlier. 'Twas exhilarating to stand there with Will, high above the world.

She faced out, away from the bailey and the keep, the reminders of her responsibilities. Looking out over the moonswept trees where Sherwood drew close to the curtain wall, Julianna could almost imagine no one else existed except her and Will.

He stood pressed close behind her, his arms round her just tight enough to hold her to him. Her hair whipped about him every so often, drawing a laugh from him that made her think he was enjoying this blustery night as much as she. His voice and laughter vibrated from him to her where his chest pressed against her back; the intimacy of that subtle touch sent a corresponding quiver of longing through her.

They'd done most of their talking now. Will's explanation of the task for his overlord had eased away her last remnants of concern about him. She understood that Will must leave and complete his charge, and believed him when he told her he would return to Tuck's Tower as soon as he could.

Though she'd ranted at him a bit over the documents he'd discovered under the hearth, she did understand why he'd been searching her chamber. In his situation, she'd likely have done the same.

As it was, she'd barely held on to her own scruples long enough to restrain herself from unsealing the missives Will had brought with him. They'd tempted her, 'twas true; now that she knew who they were intended for, she was doubly glad she hadn't broken the messages open and read them.

He was fortunate, indeed, not to have lost them when he was wandering through Sherwood, or when he'd been set upon.

'Twas fortunate she'd come along when she had, she thought, suppressing a shudder of reaction, for she doubted his attackers would have let him live.

Julianna said a silent prayer of thanks to the Virgin, both for sparing Will's life, and for bringing him into her life.

Will pushed aside her hair and brushed his lips over the side of her neck. "I saw the documents myself, but tell me, love—is it really true that the Lady Marian was the same Maid Marian of legend? And was Robin truly your father?"

A shiver of reaction spread heat through her body. Will chuckled, and repeated the caress.

She turned in his arms, just enough to see his face. "Do you really expect an answer from me— any kind at all—when you do that? Though I shouldn't tell you so, you make it nigh impossible to think."

"Good! Why should you be able to, when I cannot?" He slid his hands around her waist and drew her closer. "My poor feeble brain surrenders to other parts—" he pressed against her, making it clear what parts he meant "—and I become a mindless mass of—"

Julianna heard the distinctive twang of a bow just before an arrow whizzed toward them. "Will!" She ducked behind the wall and threw herself to the side, lunging and trying to catch hold of Will to pull him down onto the wall walk with her.

At the same instant Will moved in the opposite direction.

The hem of his tunic slipped through her hand; she kept moving. Arms flailing, she sought in vain for anything to seize hold of.

"Julianna!" Will cried as he rolled halfway off the walk and grabbed for her.

Suddenly she felt nothing but air beneath her.

"No!" Her breath caught in her throat, Julianna closed her eyes and prayed.

Chapter Nineteen

Will caught the back of Julianna's gown with one hand, bringing her fall to an abrupt halt. He slumped down onto the rough stone walkway, all his energies focused on hauling her up and over the edge before her gown could tear and send her plummeting toward the ground yet again.

He heard people running toward them, but he dared not look away from her. "Don't move, love," he said, somehow infusing his voice with calm. "I've got you, and I won't let you fall."

Someone grabbed his legs and held them still. "Here, milord, we've got you, and someone'll down below will catch milady should she fall. Let me help ye."

Will grunted his thanks and, grasping for Julianna's arm with his other hand, he slowly pulled her level with the walkway. She scrambled up and sprawled beside him, her breathing harsh, her eyes squeezed shut.

He moved to lie beside her and began to check her over for injuries.

"I'm fine!" she snarled. "Leave me alone."

Ignoring her command, he continued his inspection until he'd assured himself she'd sustained no obvious injury. "You'll likely be sore on the morrow, but it appears the arrow missed you."

Julianna sat up and cuffed him on the leg. "What did I do?"

"I thought the arrow would hit *you,* that you were going to tumble over the edge." Tears glittered in her eyes, but she didn't let them fall.

"That's a reason to hit me?" he asked, glancing at her warily. If she wanted to use him to vent her fear, he'd let her—as long as she didn't hit him in any of the places he noticed were beginning to hurt, now that his own fear for her had begun to ebb.

"Aye," she said, winding up to clout him again.

"No, you don't, love." Ignoring the audience gathering nearby, Will pulled himself to his feet, bent and hauled Julianna over his shoulder, and headed back to the keep through the path that suddenly opened for him along the walkway.

Somehow Julianna held her temper until Will carried her through the great hall, up the stairs and into her own chamber. If not for the fact that she worried she'd do him further harm—or that he might drop her—she'd have shrieked out all her fears at once.

Of course, she'd rather not do so with the audience that had followed them from the wall walk into the keep in spite of the ominous glares she sent their way.

If she heard one more person mutter about the Bride of the Tower, she'd scream!

As soon as Will closed the door and set her on her feet, however, she felt free to say whatever she wanted.

She noted that Will had moved away from her and taken a seat on the stool near the hearth—an act that infuriated her more.

"Are you afraid of me?" she demanded, knowing she sounded a shrew. However, at the moment she didn't care; she was through being the calm and reasonable Lady Julianna.

Will turned the stool and faced her directly. "Nay. Do you fear me?" he asked in a reasonable tone.

"Of course not!"

"Good." He turned his attention to kindling a fire in the hearth, ignoring the fact that she needed his attention.

She knew she was acting like a spoiled child, but that knowledge didn't calm her unreasonable temper in the slightest. "How dare you toss me over your shoulder like some barbarian knight making off with a trophy, and haul me through my own courtyard?"

Will straightened at her tartly spoken words and stared at her, his eyes narrowed. "The only place I'm likely to haul you is over my knee," he said darkly, coming to his feet and stalking across the room toward her.

Julianna backed up, but soon found herself against the wall. "What are you talking about?" He certainly had come back to life quickly. Too quickly. She'd wanted a reaction, but she hadn't expected this.

She'd meant what she'd said before, though; he didn't frighten her. She stood her ground when he placed his hands on the wall on either side of her head, trapping her in place. His eyes held her captive, dark blue and filled with some emotion she didn't recognize. There was something exciting, compelling, about his ardor. Her heart picked up its pace as she waited to see where this would lead them.

"Do you have any idea how I felt when I heard the arrow, when I saw you tumble off the wall?" he asked, his voice low.

Will's intensity made the fear she'd felt at the time return full force. She couldn't force a single word through the sudden thickness blocking her throat, so she shook her head.

"With my bare hands I could have killed the bastard who shot at you. 'Twas a miracle you weren't harmed." Closing his eyes, Will leaned forward until his face rested against hers. "By the Virgin, Julianna—my duty to Lord Rannulf, the messages for the king's men—none of it mattered. All I could see was your face. For a moment I feared I couldn't save you." Groaning, he wrapped her in his arms.

Will held her as though she were as delicate as glass, the fine tremor of his body an indication of his feelings. Her heart full, Julianna closed her arms around him, at first to give him comfort, and then because she couldn't bear to let him go.

This was what she'd needed, what she'd craved, since the moment he'd told her he would be leaving Tuck's Tower. The security of Will's embrace, the solid feel of his strong, lean body pressed against her.

Nothing and no one could harm her when he held her in his arms.

The tension in Will's body changed, became more powerful, more sensual. Julianna drew away from him, far enough to look into his eyes. They held a dark passion she didn't quite understand.

But far from fearing it, Julianna rejoiced in it, for she could not mistake his intent. His aim no longer to give comfort, now he embraced her as a lover, the weight of him along her body a caress.

"Julianna, I need you," he whispered, his lips brushing her ear as his hands slipped urgently along her ribs. A shiver ran down her spine, the sensation deepening when his hands stopped just below her breasts.

His palms spread their heat along her flesh, making her yearn for his hands to slide a little higher to soothe the ache they'd started. Meeting his gaze again, she put her hands over his and boldly guided them to rest where she ached most.

Will dragged his mouth over her neck, again and again, as his fingers curled about her softness.

Julianna was glad to be leaning against the wall, for her legs could scarcely hold her. Heat radiated from Will's hands, burning through her to settle and build deep within her body. She clung to him, all her senses focused where they touched, on what they were doing. If a herd of cattle had run through her chamber at that moment, she'd not have noticed.

Or cared.

When he finally kissed her, she couldn't help but moan her pleasure. Will's lips curled into a smile against her mouth. "Ah, love—tell me—" he said, continuing to tempt, to tease her by drawing his tongue along her lips, then dueling with hers in a thrust and parry echoed by their bodies "—*please* tell me you want me as much as I want you."

She dragged her mouth from his, the drugging warmth of his kisses sapping her will to resist, while also imbuing her with the power to meet Will's desire with equal intensity.

He reached down and swept her into his arms, carrying her to her bed with surprising ease.

"Put me down," Julianna whispered against his neck. "I cannot believe you're 'hauling me about' again. Do you want me to have to sew you up a second time?"

"Now *that* would be an unusual method of heating my blood." He chuckled. "From some mysterious country in the East, mayhap? We'll pass on that practice, don't you agree?" He shifted her so that she rode higher in his arms and could help hold herself up.

"Aye—I found nothing enticing about it at the time, I'm afraid, save for the fact that I got to stare at your naked chest," she added with a grin.

The saltiness of his skin distracted her; she dragged her tongue along the strong cords of his neck and up to his now-smooth chin, giggling when he growled low in his throat and dipped his arms as if he meant to drop her. "Don't you dare!" she shrieked. She clutched his shoulders and clung to him.

His lips never left hers until he laid her on the mattress and followed her down onto the bed, both of them gasping, breathless with the force of their desire.

He tugged the bed curtains wide, until the tall candle beside the bed bathed them in its soft glow. The light brought out the fire in his blue eyes, heating her blood and sharpening her senses. "I want to see you," he whispered in her ear. "I want you to see me."

Oh, how she wanted that as well!

Patience, she told herself. Soon he'd be hers; he'd teach her what she'd yearned to know from the moment she'd met him.

All she'd wanted since the first time they'd kissed.

Will slipped her gown and undertunic from her, following the fabric with his hands.

The smooth fabric of her silk chemise brushed against her sensitized flesh, magnifying every movement of Will's fingers along the length of her body. Her golden medallion rested in the valley between her breasts, absorbing the heat from her flesh and making her more aware of her femininity.

Will sat back on his heels beside her and raised the hem of her chemise, up her past her knees to her thighs, bending to drag his mouth over her skin as he uncovered it, inch by tortuous inch.

He paused with the fabric pooled at the top of

her thighs. "Your legs are so lovely, so strong," he whispered, glancing up and meeting her eyes as he swept both hands beneath the cool silk, teasing her as his fingers moved ever closer to the curls covering the heart of her desire.

Julianna reached for him, wanting to draw him close enough so she could touch him as well, but he caught her hand in his. "Will—"

"Nay, love. If you touch me now, I'll be done so fast I'll embarrass myself." He leaned over her and captured both her hands in his, threading his fingers with hers so they were palm to palm. "Let me pleasure you," he murmured. "You'll have your chance at me soon enough, I promise you."

"Not soon enough for me," she protested before thought and words fled in the wake of Will's touch.

He brought her right hand to his lips, nibbling at her fingertips and drawing his tongue over the sensitive skin of her wrist. Traveling up her arm, when he reached her shoulder he switched his attention to her other hand and repeated the caress.

Each scrape of teeth and tongue thrummed within her, heating her body, making her ache for his touch in other places. By the time he reached her left shoulder, she could swear she'd melted into the sheets.

The urge to touch *him* had grown until 'twas only the fact that he still held her hands that kept her from pulling him down to her. "Is it my turn now?" she asked, her voice little more than a purr. "I need to touch you, so much."

He drew her hands up over her head and slowly released them. "Keep them there," he told her. When she would have reached for him, he shook his head and moved her hands back, closing them about the silken bed curtains. "'Twill be better if you leave them there, Julianna." He nuzzled aside her hair, the brush of his own tousled locks along her neck a tantalizing sensation. "Trust me, love. I'll make you fly."

Chapter Twenty

His mouth painted a line of heat down her throat. When he reached her bosom he paused, nuzzled aside her necklace, then bent to nip at her breast through the sheer material. "You wouldn't believe how many times I've imagined you like this," he said, looking up at her and smiling as he drew her chemise higher, until it caught just below her breasts.

Though she lay exposed from the waist down, surprisingly she felt no embarrassment. Instead she rejoiced in the brush of his fiery gaze over her aching flesh. "If I cannot touch you, at least touch me. I need to feel your skin against mine. Now," she commanded.

Will's teasing smile, his expression as he continued to look at her, sent a shiver of anticipation through her. "Do you, my heart?" He slipped his hands up her arms and drew her chemise over her breasts—slowly, the soft silk an almost unbearable pleasure as it rasped over her nipples. "For now I just want to see you."

Will raised her up enough to slide the silk over her head, then laid her back against the pillows, her arms still above her head. Garbed only in her gold necklace, she felt wanton, womanly, beautiful.

"You, sir, are a tease. I believe you delight in torturing me."

"Are you complaining?" he asked. "Let me torment you more." He ran his hands through the length of her hair, arranging it so it moved over her flesh as she shifted beneath his attentions. He brushed a finger over her cheekbone and down to her chin, skating lightly around her lips and making the sensitive flesh nigh hum with anticipation.

Julianna captured his fingertip with her teeth and set out to tease *him*. He sat still, eyes dark and heated and fixed upon hers, as she nipped at his fingertip, swept her tongue over it with slow caresses and finally drew it into her mouth.

He groaned and closed his eyes, permitting the

caress for a moment longer before sliding his hand away.

Down her neck and over her breast.

To settle over her most sensitive flesh. She gasped as the moisture from his finger sent a trail of fire streaking from her breasts to her womanhood. He stroked her aching flesh, watching her all the while, till it took all her will to remain still.

'Twas all she could do to obey Will and not reach out for him, to drive him to madness as he'd already done to her.

"You are so beautiful," he murmured. Sitting back, he untied his shirt one-handed, his other hand still ministering to her aching body. His gaze was like the touch of his hand, stroking and heating her flesh to an unbearable pitch.

By the time he'd shrugged free of his shirt, Julianna was ready to rip it from him herself. "Now?" she demanded.

"Aye, love, now," he growled.

Her hands met him halfway as he leaned down to kiss her again, coming up to brush over the firm muscles and rake through the mat of dark blond curls. His indrawn breath gave her the courage to skim her fingertips over the corded expanse of his stomach, then work at untying his braes.

Passion made her clumsy, so that Will ended up unknotting the string himself. He guided her hands to his waist, however, and slid them into the loosened fabric.

She didn't push the leggings off just yet, however, for she'd a torment of her own to carry out. Cupping his buttocks beneath the garment, she stroked his lean body, sliding her hands around his hips, but never quite touching his manhood.

"Julianna, do you want me?" She raked her fingernails over his stomach; he dragged in a breath and captured her hands, holding them still. "We don't have to make love—I can still give you pleasure."

His words cut through the cloud of passion that surrounded her. There was no turning back—but she didn't *want* to turn back from wherever they were headed. So long as she and Will went there together, she'd be content with that.

But not quite yet, she decided with a devilish smile. She slid her hands free of his hold and set about driving him mad.

Will groaned as Julianna's fingertips skimmed over his aching flesh, returning to slip inside the soft, worn braes and linger there. He felt warm, exciting beneath her touch, and the sounds of pleasure he made fired her own passion.

He didn't remain a passive participant for long. He lavished her breasts with attention, his hands and mouth never still. Julianna's body felt light, warm, passion-lit until 'twas a wonder she didn't explode into a thousand shards of light.

They teased each other until their bodies were slick with sweat, until Julianna could not bear to be apart from Will a moment longer. "Now," she pleaded.

Once again he covered her hand with his own, pressing her fingers more firmly along his length. "Are you sure, Julianna? Be very certain this is what you want—that I'm what you want." Holding her gaze, he pressed himself into her hand. "Because once I've got you, I won't let you go."

"You cannot stop me now," she told him. "Not if my life depended on it." Smiling, Julianna slipped her hands into his braes and pushed them off. "I'm not going anywhere," she said. She leaned over him, her hands running boldly over his hair-roughened flesh. "And neither are you."

Groaning deep in his chest, Will moved onto

his side, caressing her with his eyes. Her body quivered in response, fired by an almost unbearable yearning to feel him against her skin, his weight pressing her into the soft bed beneath her, to know the strength of his passion burning hot within her.

She got her wish. His every movement exquisitely slow, Will positioned her beneath him and linked his hands with hers. "Be mine, Julianna," he whispered, his gaze holding hers. "Make me yours." He eased into her body, allowing her time to adjust to him.

She felt a mere twinge of discomfort as he slid into her, then passion sent her flying.

Watching him, she matched move for move, using her hands and body to tempt him, even as he did the same to her. Soon both were gasping.

Her hands skimming the sweat-damp contours of Will's back, Julianna's entire being strained toward an elusive pinnacle. The higher she climbed, the more tantalizing it seemed, but she couldn't quite—

"Easy, love." Will groaned into her mouth just before his tongue slipped in to duel with hers. "Don't rush—'tis better if we go slow."

"I will if you will," she told him. Capturing

his face in her hands, she drew her fingers through his hair and down his chest. His entire body tightened in response; grinning, he varied the rhythm of their bodies, continuing to taunt and tease. Every motion a caress, he reached down and repositioned her legs higher about his waist, tearing his lips free with a gasp as he sank more deeply into her softness.

The intensity of Will's gaze, the urgency of his body, finally pushed Julianna over the edge. Sinking her teeth into his shoulder, her entire being reaching for him, she flew beyond the boundaries of pleasure.

Breathless, unable to do more than grasp Will to her as if she'd never let him go, Julianna's head fell back on the pillows.

But he wasn't done with her yet. The flush of passion on his cheekbones matched the drive of his straining body, fiery, hot. Arms unsteady, Will rested his weight on his elbows and clasped her face in his hands. "Mine," he said in the ghost of a whisper. The smooth grace of his movements disappeared. "Julianna," he ground out as the pleasure took him captive and pulled her along with it.

Stifling a moan against his lips, she grabbed

him tightly just before pleasure sent her flying again, as well.

A quiet rapping on the door drew Will up from the depths of sleep at once. He slid carefully away from Julianna, who slept on, apparently oblivious to the disturbance.

He realized he was naked just before he got to the door. Where had his braes gone?

He grabbed the end of a sheet from the bed and eased it away from Julianna, who still didn't move. What he and Julianna had been doing would be clear to whoever stood on the other side of the portal, no matter what he did—or didn't—wear.

What if Julianna didn't want anyone to know she'd given herself to a man? She was a noble lady, after all.

Jesu, at this point he could scarce think straight; no matter what he did, he'd likely be wrong.

More knocking, a bit louder this time, spurred his brain. He'd simply pretend he'd been in the other chamber, asleep on his pallet where he no doubt ought to be.

Will hurried into the other room and quietly shut the connecting door. Yawning, he gathered the sheet about his waist and tugged open his own.

Rolf turned to him, eyes narrowed suspiciously. "I was seeking my lady, not you," he told Will.

"Since it didn't seem as though Lady Julianna was about to respond to your summons, I decided to see who was here and what they wanted. After she nearly fell off the wall tonight, I imagine she's resting." Will scratched absently at his chest and met Rolf's steady gaze. "No doubt she needs it."

The man nodded, though he didn't look too eager to deal with Will rather than Lady Julianna.

"If you want to wake her, all you need to do is to hammer a bit louder," Will informed him. "I'm sure she'll awaken eventually."

"Nay, it'll wait till morn. Just wanted to let her know we couldn't find the archer who shot at you. We'll keep looking." Rolf turned away as if to leave, then spun about and took a step closer to Will, his face twisted into a scowl. "If you seek to hide what you and milady've been doing, I suggest you put on a shirt next time you come to the door." His frown disappeared, replaced by a grin, to Will's surprise. "Doesn't matter much which door you open, when you look like you've been marked up by a she-cat."

Will glanced down at his chest, where the marks of Julianna's stitchery had been joined by obvious scratches on his shoulder and a love bite low on his throat. *So much for subtlety.* He nodded.

Rolf thumped him on the arm. "You just remember to treat her well, young sir, else you'll be answering to more than just me." This time when he turned away, he kept on going down the stairs.

Will climbed back into bed and watched Julianna as she slept, her hair spread out over the pillows, the ends draped across his chest. 'Twas as soft and sweet as her skin, a temptation he already wanted to indulge himself in again.

But though his body might be willing, his mind knew he'd other things to do, more important in the greater scheme of things than to lie abed with his lover and fill his senses with her.

She turned toward him and nestled closer. He shifted his wounded arm so her head rested on his shoulder, even that slight movement reminding him of the injuries Julianna had mended.

His head felt fine now—because 'twas hard as a rock, no doubt, as Lord Connor and Lord Rannulf both had reminded him so often. The other wounds appeared to be healing well, but he'd put a strain on them by pulling Julianna up and onto the wall walk.

And by hauling her back to her chamber over his shoulder, he thought with a quiet laugh.

Not to mention the new "wounds" he bore— wounds he'd wear proudly, for they were the marks of a woman well satisfied.

He couldn't distract himself from the night's earlier events for long, however. They'd no doubt haunt his dreams for years to come. That moment when he'd grabbed for Julianna's gown, had feared the delicate fabric would tear completely and send her plunging to the hard earth below....

He'd have reached for her had it torn his wounds open wide; protecting himself at her expense had never crossed his mind. How could he have watched her fall and done nothing? The mere thought was nigh impossible to contemplate. Though a fall from that height would not necessarily have killed her, of a certainty she'd have been gravely injured.

Thank God he'd been able to keep hold of her!

The recollection alone of those endless moments was enough to send shivers down his spine.

Something cold brushed against his chest, startling him from the disquieting memory. 'Twas Julianna's medallion. He leaned closer to peer at the design etched there; 'twas of an archer drawing back his bow.

Robin's daughter, indeed.

She'd her father's bravery, Will knew; seldom did women go so far as to actually protect their lands with their own bodies. Even Gillian, for all her bold ways, had never ridden about her demesne fully armed in a warrior's armor, ready to fight.

Julianna stretched, rubbing against him from head to toe. His body leapt instantly to attention.

"Will?" she mumbled, still half-asleep.

"Aye, love, I'm here."

She smiled and pressed an awkward kiss on his chin before burrowing under the covers. He wrapped her in his arms and rested his head atop hers.

How was it that he suddenly understood what had made so many of the men he knew become husbands as well as warriors? Had it happened so quickly as this, made them question themselves, their lives, their emotions?

He'd not ever expected anything to tug him

away from his duty. He'd planned out his life. There had been the possibility of a mate, of a home and children—but as the next step a man took, not as a compulsion that drove him, as his growing feelings for Julianna were doing.

He *must* leave for Lincoln today! If he was well enough to make love to Julianna, he could certainly mount a horse and go about the business that had brought him here in the first place.

Though he couldn't complete all he'd set out to do when he'd come to Nottinghamshire, not quite yet, he reminded himself. His reservations about Birkland and Sir Richard Belleville would have to wait until he returned from Lincoln.

He could—and would—send word to Lord Rannulf about his suspicions, however, especially since he didn't plan to return to l'Eau Clair quite yet.

Now that he knew Rachel was Belleville's sister, he wondered if she could be useful in discovering what her brother was doing. Perhaps she knew already.... He glanced down at the woman held snug in his embrace. Mayhap Julianna might be able to learn something from Rachel while he was gone. From what Julianna had told him last night, Rachel had no desire to return to her brother's keeping, and she had lived at Birkland.

She might be a treasure trove of information, if she was willing to share it.

If he could arrange for her to go to one of Lord Rannulf's keeps, perhaps to join Gillian's household...

That might work.

Will brushed at something tickling his neck, and captured Julianna's hand. Giggling, she rolled atop him and drew the fingers of her other hand around his neck to hover at his throat.

"I've been attacked by a she-cat, or so I was told," he said. "Can you see the marks?"

Color bloomed in her cheeks as she stroked the mark on his throat, then covered it with her palm. "Someone saw? Who was it?"

"Aye." He eased her other hand around from his neck and stroked it over the scratches. "He saw these as well," he told her teasingly.

Julianna pressed both hands palm-down on his chest and raised herself up. "Who, Will?" she coaxed, bending to trace her tongue over the mark on his throat.

He laughed at the expression on her face—concentration mixed with blossoming passion. "What will you do if I don't tell you?'' he asked, his voice thickening as she scraped her teeth lightly along his collarbone.

''I may be forced to have my way with you until you talk,'' she murmured. She settled atop his burgeoning manhood and held him cradled against her softness. Her breasts grazed his chest, her nipples tracing a heated path across his own.

Will sucked in a shaky breath. ''Is that supposed to make me talk?'' he teased. ''''Tis more like to strike me dumb, especially if you continue what you're doing.'' He smoothed his hands down over her back and cupped her buttocks to hold her tight to his aching flesh. ''Please, love, don't stop what you're doing.''

Julianna smiled and pressed her mouth to his own eager lips. ''Sir Will, prepare to be tortured.''

Chapter Twenty-One

Birkland

He couldn't have received better news.

Sir Richard rubbed his hands together, his pleasure at the report from Tuck's Tower the one highpoint in a truly miserable week. His archer had not only been able to take a clear shot at Julianna the night before, it sounded as though he'd hit her!

Richard doubted there would be much resistance at all from her people once he brought his troops in to take command of the place.

His hands shook with excitement as he poured a generous measure of wine into a heavy chased goblet. 'Twas a fine brew, worthy of the occasion.

Now if only the man he'd sent to bring back Rachel would return with her soon, he might finally allow himself to believe that all his plans would soon come to a successful fruition.

By Christ, but he was tired of the need to plot and scheme! The continuous struggle to gain the power he deserved sucked away the enjoyment of his victories, both large and small. He never seemed to have a moment of peace to savor them.

Richard stared into the deep red wine, the color of pleasure, of wealth and richness. Someday, he vowed, someday soon he would garb himself in crimson velvet, savor the finest drink, partake of exotic foods and have the most skilled and beautiful highborn harlots at his beck and call.

The whores who serviced him now would do nigh anything he ordered, 'twas true, but he'd heard that there were noble women—beautiful and experienced—who took pleasure in his sort of love play.

Women who'd satisfy his every desire with equal fervor.

Everything he'd ever wanted.

Soon, he reminded himself.

He sipped the last of the wine, rolling the rich vintage over his tongue.

Very, very soon.

Tuck's Tower

Julianna awoke alone, though she hadn't far to look to find her lover. Will stood by the window, gazing past the open shutters at the rising sun.

She sat up and swung her legs over the edge of the bed, the better to savor the sight of him. His hair and skin gleamed with a golden glow, limned by dawn's light. The increasing brightness highlighted the lean musculature of his body.

The body she'd learned by sight, by touch, by taste last night.

As he had learned hers.

"If you're to leave today, you'll need your messages back." Wrapping a sheet about her, Julianna climbed out of bed and went to the hearth. "You were very close when you found those old parchments." She knelt and tugged at several stones, opening up a narrow space. Reaching in, she eased out the leather pouch and held it out for him. He took it and set it on the bed near his discarded clothes.

"I apologize for reading the one addressed to

Sir Richard,'' Julianna said. '''Twas none of my business, I know. 'Tis only that the man infuriates me! He's a boil on the backside of Nottingham-shire, though since your overlord lives far from here, I can understand why he wouldn't know Richard's true nature. He's an avaricious fool. I hope your Lord Rannulf will remove him from Birkland and send someone else to oversee the place.''

''What little I saw of him didn't impress me, either. 'Tis another reason Lord Rannulf sent me to deliver messages to the overseers of his hold-ings—he wanted to know how they went on.''

'''Tis a sensible plan.'' Julianna shifted to sit on the low hearth. ''And an immense responsi-bility. Lord Rannulf must trust you very much.''

Will seemed to be uncomfortable with her words, but he nodded. ''I hope he does. I've done my best to fulfill his expectations—and my own. I don't wish to remain a landless knight forever.''

She doubted he would, since he obviously worked hard to perform his duties.

He stretched, then winced.

''Do your wounds still pain you?'' she asked. She rose and went to stand behind him, wrapping her arms about him and pressing her cheek to the smooth, strong flesh of his back.

Will turned within her embrace. "A bit." He rested his brow against hers while she checked the bandages for bleeding or seepage. "They're fine, only a little sore—from yesterday's events, no doubt," he added with a teasing smile.

"I'm not surprised," Julianna agreed. "'Tis a wonder you're not back in bed, suffering the effects of doing too much too soon."

"If I'd the time, 'twould be my fondest wish to climb back into bed—as long as you were there with me." He swept the tangled mass of her hair from her face. "Though the worst ache I'm suffering at the moment isn't covered by a bandage, nor would it benefit from that hog swill Dora gave me."

Quite aware of just what ache Will referred to—how could she not notice his swollen manhood pressing urgently against her?—Julianna felt a sudden wave of shyness. She focused her attention instead upon tightening the knot of the bandage wrapped about his arm. "What would ease you, then? A different potion, or an unguent?" she teased, trailing her fingers fleetingly over his belly and the rigid flesh below.

Will caught her hand and drew it away from such dangerous territory. "You, Julianna." He kissed her fingers, then pressed them over his heart. "You're all the medicine I need, love. Kiss me and make me whole." Leaning over her, he cupped her chin in his palm and captured her lips.

Julianna kissed him back with all the intensity of a perfect moment shared, drinking of his mouth with a hunger she knew only he could satisfy. When Will held her, she felt as though anything was possible, even those things she'd feared.

He didn't seem to mind her manner of dress, her habit of wearing sword and dagger, the fact that she commanded Tuck's Tower. She could even believe it might be possible to share that authority.

With Will.

He gave her a gift, something she had learned not to expect from any man other than her father.

He treated her as an equal, with respect.

Yet he also treated her as a woman—cherished, appreciated.

The way he made her feel right now.

Julianna wished this moment would never end, even as she knew it must. The sun shone full upon them; 'twas nearly time for Will to leave, and for her to go about her usual tasks.

Before she could break away from him, he

grasped her hands and raised them to his lips. "Let me say goodbye to you now, love." His eyes darkened, the blue intense, his expression solemn, sincere. "I'll return as soon as I can, I swear to you." He turned over her right hand, tracing his lips across her callused palm. "And I'll not leave you again unless you wish me gone. Friend or lover—whichever you want of me, I shall be."

A rueful smile on his lips, he stepped away from her, exposing his swollen manhood. "Though it must be clear to you which I'd rather you choose."

Her choice as well.

Julianna thought of many things she should say, but 'twas difficult to force the words past the lump of sorrow clogging her throat. "Godspeed," she whispered as Will gathered up his clothing and message pouch and, with one last smile, left.

Julianna watched from her window as Will, escorted by two of her men-at-arms, rode out of Tuck's Tower. A sense of panic seized her—what if he never returned? He'd already been attacked not far from here; would the men she'd sent to accompany him be enough of a guard should he be attacked again?

What if he decided he'd no reason to come back? Would his desire for her, so quickly evident and so swiftly satisfied, fade away as rapidly as the leagues passed beneath his mount's flying hooves?

Despite their recent intimacy, what did she truly know about Will Bowman?

What if she had traded her virginity—freely given, no mistake—for a moment's fleeting pleasure?

Did that diminish the pleasure they'd shared, lessen the significance of the unspoken commitment she'd made to Will by making love with him?

What if, what if…? Tears welling in her eyes, she turned from the window once the gates had creaked closed. She'd drive herself mad if she lingered on this path, for it led nowhere. She had no answers for the multitude of questions that plagued her, now that 'twas too late to ask them.

Assuming she'd have had the courage to ask.

There were times, she knew, when 'twas better to simply let some questions stay unspoken. She'd been taught never to ask about anything unless she wanted an honest answer.

Sometimes, though, perhaps 'twas better to remain ignorant of the truth. Though that had never been her way, it held a certain appeal, especially today. Her emotions felt flayed raw, and her usual confidence had apparently fled along with her innocence.

Enough! she chided herself. Only time could provide the answers she sought. In the meantime she ought to be able to distract herself.

Julianna stooped to pick up the torn remnants of her once-beautiful gown. Though she was no seamstress, she doubted the garment could be salvaged.

She traced her fingers over the few pearls left round the neckline, saddened by the loss of yet another remnant of her mother's love. Holding the soft silk to her cheek, she breathed in the faint, comforting scent of her mother's perfume and reminded herself that she saw the tangible signs of her mother's love every day. A secure home; a loving father; the loyalty of her people to her, and to her parents'—*all* three of her parents'—memories.

Lady Marian had provided well for her daughter, left her well protected by both her fathers' people, for the aging remnants of Robin's band

and their families resided in the village beyond the walls of Tuck's Tower.

Thankfully, a knock at the door forced Julianna to abandon her futile musings. "Come," she called, remembering at the last moment to wrap herself more securely in the sheet she'd pulled off the bed.

Rachel paused just inside the open door. "Lady Julianna—"

"Please, come in and shut the door." Julianna set the gown she'd been holding onto the bed. "As you can see, I'm not dressed enough to leave the door open just yet."

Rachel did as she'd requested, but still lingered on the other side of the chamber.

"Is something wrong?" Julianna asked.

The other woman clasped her hands in front of her as though she were a penitent—a most unusual attitude for "Mary," though mayhap a typical one for Rachel, for all Julianna knew about her.

"Rachel?"

"Lady Julianna, now that you know who I am—and in light of yesterday's humiliating debacle—I'm not sure where I belong here at Tuck's Tower." She glanced up at Juliana and drew a deep breath, seeming to draw confidence from something she saw. "Am I still a servant, or something more? Or would you rather I simply leave Tuck's Tower altogether and return to my brother?"

Shame washed over Julianna. She'd completely ignored the fact that Rachel was not a servant after all—and everything that revelation meant to her status at Tuck's Tower.

How could she have neglected to see to Rachel's safety? "I'm so sorry, Rachel! My mind was obviously elsewhere, since I did so little to reassure you or to provide for you."

"You'd been ill, milady. You'd other things on your mind than me."

Julianna's shame deepened. "Sweet Mary save you, where did you sleep last night?" she asked, envisioning Rachel curled up with the hounds on the rush-strewn floor of the great hall.

"I returned to the barracks," Rachel said impassively. "I knew I could trust the men-at-arms to protect me for another night, and my belongings were there. Anyway those witches who went after me yesterday heard an earful from Rolf and Diccon about what they did. So I don't think they'll be after me again anytime soon." She reached for the knife sheath hanging from her belt. "Besides, Diccon found me a dagger. I'm not afraid to use it if I need to."

Considering the state Rachel had been in when Julianna put a stop to the commotion in the bailey, 'twas astounding that she should be so composed now. Of course, unlike the previous day, no one was threatening Rachel's life. Still, Rachel clearly possessed a calmer nature, and a more forgiving one, than her brother did.

It was their good fortune 'twas so, for one Sir Richard Belleville was enough to manage.

"You are no longer a servant, Rachel," Julianna told her. "Unless you wish to be of service to us here at Tuck's Tower by making use of your skills as a healer to keep us all well."

"'Twould be my pleasure, Lady Julianna." Rachel bowed her head in acknowledgment. "I thank you."

"Nay, I owe you my gratitude for agreeing to stay." Julianna crossed to the door of the storeroom and tugged it open. "We shall set up this chamber for you, if you'd like. You'll be safer here from Joan and her ilk—and your character less maligned, as well."

Rachel joined her and peered into the darkened

chamber. "'Tis too much, milady!" Yet Julianna heard excitement in the other woman's voice, and anticipation. "But I'll take it, and gladly."

How had Rachel's brother and sister treated her, that she should be so filled with enthusiasm by a storeroom?

"'Tis settled then. I'll send for someone to help you arrange it as you see fit."

Julianna left Rachel to focus on her new chamber, glad to have her own room to herself. She needed to wash and dress, to ready herself for the coming day.

A day empty of Will.

Until recently, all her days had passed with her completely unaware of Will's existence. She ought to be capable of managing without him now.

Now, however, she knew what had been missing from her life. How would she get by if he didn't return?

Half-dressed, worried, Julianna knelt by her bed and prayed she'd never need to find out.

Chapter Twenty-Two

Lincoln

Will had never been so happy to leave a battle ground as he was to leave the siege at Lincoln— and he hadn't even bloodied his sword!

But to have finally carried out his duty was an enormous relief, especially once the earl of Pembroke reassured him that the delay in delivering the messages had not resulted in anyone's death, or the destruction of important plans.

After seizing but one night's rest to break their journey, Will and his two escorts took to the road once again, spurring their mounts on to Tuck's Tower in spite of their weariness.

Will could not elude the feeling that something

was about to go wrong, if it hadn't already. He wished he hadn't left Julianna alone, though what good he might be to her, he didn't know.

But to be with her once more... He felt so strong a sense of loss without Julianna by his side, he knew he would do whatever necessary to remain a part of her life.

He'd already begun to set things in motion so he could shift the focus of his life, from his service to Lord Rannulf to a new life within Julianna's milieu. He'd sent word to Lord Rannulf, asking to be released from his service—and telling him of the situation at Birkland, of the attack and any other information he thought might be useful.

Pembroke had been most generous with his advice, once Will got up the nerve to ask for it. He'd been interested in what information Will had about Sir Richard, although according to Pembroke, Belleville was but a tiny, unimpressive minnow who assumed himself powerful enough to swim with the sharks.

Still, considering the fact that Julianna believed Belleville to be a threat of some kind, Will scraped together what information he could about the man. It might be useful to her.

Or rather to them, for he refused to leave her to face that threat—nay, *any* threat—alone.

For the first time since he'd been a child, a sense of anticipation spurred Will on, making him impatient to return home.

He'd never have anticipated that home would be a place he hadn't known existed a week ago.

Or that he'd be so eager because of a woman.

Lady Julianna d'Arcy, the woman he already realized he couldn't live without.

Tuck's Tower

The past several days—since Will had left—seemed an eternity to Julianna. Although she'd been busy, catching up on all she'd ignored once she'd brought Will to Tuck's Tower, as well as preparing for what she considered the inevitable encounter with Sir Richard, time dragged by at a snail's pace.

And the nights were unending, sleepless and filled with worry and apprehension. Julianna felt locked into a particularly hellish form of limbo—waiting, always waiting.

For Belleville to attack; for her uncle to arrive

at her door to drag her away to the nigh-cloistered life of a noble lady; for Will's return.

One of the few good things to come of the wait was that Julianna and Rachel had become friends.

Rachel was a decent woman, intelligent and well schooled in a lady's ways, yet not possessed of a high-and-mighty attitude.

She'd never have managed to remain with the men in the barracks for long if that had been her way, Julianna thought with a wry laugh.

She'd progressed from pondering "what ifs" to hearing a constant litany of "what to dos" echoing through her head. Though she couldn't decide if that was progress, or if she were simply losing her mind, at least 'twas a different refrain.

Sooner or later the tension that held them within its grasp must break.

Soon, Julianna reassured herself. Something had to happen soon.

Birkland

Johan grinned and settled himself atop a comfortable pile of hay. 'Twas the first time he'd ever been so eager to see Belleville. O' course, this time he had just what Sir Richard had been wanting—oddments of information he'd collected at Tuck's Tower, valuable snippets that'd bring a smile to Belleville's face and put a pile o' coin in his own hand.

He always enjoyed getting paid, and this time Belleville had no reason whatsoever to withhold what he owed Johan.

He picked at his nails with the needle-sharp tip of his dirk, recalling how easy it had been to find out what he'd wanted. All it had taken was a bit of a romance with one of the lowliest maidservants. A few sweet words and some personal attention, he thought, his grin widening in remembrance, and he'd not only gained the knowledge he'd sought, but he'd had a ripe old time of it with the randy wench as well. Once he got what he needed from her, he'd been able to slip his blade into her heart as easily as he'd slid himself into her delightful body.

'Twas a shame he'd had to kill her, really, for she'd satisfied him well right up to the end.

"What is it this time?" Sir Richard snarled, putting an end to Johan's pleasant memories.

Despite his own eagerness, Johan took his time getting to his feet and crossing the stable to join Belleville. Wouldn't do to appear in too much of a hurry. Besides, he might as well get what amusement he could from watching Sir Richard squirm with impatience; he thought of it as an additional benefit of doing business with the arrogant bastard.

"Well, milord, I got news for ye."

"Tell me." Belleville, hands clenched into fists at his sides, waited with a surprising patience.

At least the fool hadn't grabbed for him as soon as he got there this time, Johan noted. Mayhap Belleville had finally begun to learn some manners.

"Do ye want the good news first, or the bad? I got both." Johan scratched his beard and squinted at Belleville as though weighing how much he should say. 'Twas usually good for a bit more coin if he could raise the customer's expectations a mite. "Or I could tell ye whichever ye prefer, if ye don't want 'em both."

"Christ's bones, do you never simply answer a question?" Sir Richard demanded.

Judging that Belleville was in no mood to be toyed with, Johan sighed and settled down to business. "If I tell ye all o' what I learned, ye'll have to pay me what ye still owe from the last time, as well as my usual fee. Otherwise I might forget to tell ye everythin'," he pointed out, grinning.

He could see Sir Richard's frustration mount. He had him, Johan crowed silently. This time he had him.

Taking his time, Belleville unclenched his fists and reached for the money pouch hanging from his belt. "You're naught but a thief," he complained before finally handing over the bag.

"You wouldn't have much use for me otherwise," Johan agreed. He buried his excitement and hefted the pouch in his hand before tugging open the drawstring and pouring the contents into his palm. "Seems 'bout right to me," he said with a nod. He poured the coin back into the bag and tied it to his belt. "So which do ye want first, milord—the good news, or the bad?"

"It doesn't much matter," Sir Richard said, sounding dispirited.

"I'll leave ye to decide which is which," Johan told him, feeling generous now that he'd been paid. "'Tis like this—Lady Julianna still lives, hale and healthy. Seems your archer missed her altogether. She's had company all this while, which I'll venture ye didn't know. Interestin' company."

"Who is it then, damn you?" Sir Richard demanded.

Johan savored the sensation of power over Belleville for a brief moment. Then, laughing, he relented. "Seems Bowman's been right under our noses since the attack. I found your sister Rachel, as well," he said. "Guess she decided not to go stay with your sister after all. They've each been at Tuck's Tower all along, milord."

Belleville's face darkened. "By Christ's toes," he cried. "How can that be?" After a moment, however, the tension seemed to pour out of him. "Are they both still there?" he asked, his expression and voice smooth, calm. "Tell me more."

As Johan related what he'd learned, Belleville began to pace, his expression cunning. Once Johan had finished, Sir Richard settled back against the wall and folded his arms. "Do you know, perhaps this might work to my best advantage after all. If Bowman is gone, I needn't concern myself with him for the moment, and with my sister there...it presents countless possibilities. Come, help me decide what to do."

Intrigued by this side of Sir Richard, Johan joined him, tamping down his excitement at the opportunity to help with Belleville's latest scheme.

There'd be coin in this for certain.

Lots of it, and he'd not have to share it with anyone else.

Sir Richard glanced back over his shoulder. Johan followed his gaze; they were alone in the stable, though this far back, the shadows were so deep that likely no one would notice them anyway.

"Do ye have a plan, milord?" Johan asked.

"Of course I do," Belleville told him. "But we cannot speak so loud." He motioned for Johan to move closer still.

Intrigued, Johan complied, leaning toward Belleville so he might hear.

Belleville hit him in the stomach, so hard that Johan didn't realize he'd been stabbed until he glimpsed the gore-stained dagger clutched in Belleville's fist.

He pressed his hands to his stomach, felt the hot rush of his lifeblood pouring over them as the rest of his body went cold. To his surprise he felt little pain.

"Fool!" Belleville hissed. "As if I need the likes of you to help me decide what to do."

Johan's legs folded beneath him and he slumped onto the pile of hay. He moved one hand away from his belly and managed to close it about the hilt of his knife.

Belleville knelt beside him and fumbled at the knotted string that tied the bag of coin to Johan's belt.

The thieving knave! Now he knew why Belleville had paid him so well. He must have planned all along to kill him and take back the money.

Rage gave Johan the impetus he needed to tug free his weapon and shove it toward Belleville.

As soon as the blade met flesh, he felt his last bit of strength ebb away.

But his lips twisted into one final mocking leer; the surprised expression on Sir Richard's face would be Johan's last sight before he descended into Hell.

He only hoped he took the treacherous bastard with him.

Chapter Twenty-Three

Tuck's Tower

The sound of shouting dragged Julianna from dreams of Will.

Climbing from her bed, she groped her way to the window and pushed aside the shutter. 'Twas just before dawn; the sky held a strange glow, as though the light of the rising sun had been filtered through a piece of blood red silk.

The ruckus seemed to be coming from outside the castle walls. Tossing on a shirt and leggings and thrusting her feet into her boots, Julianna snatched up her sword belt and weapons from the chest at the foot of the bed and hurried from the chamber.

She ran across the dark, empty bailey to the gatehouse and raced up the stairs. Rolf stood by the arrow slit in the front of the small room. She joined him and looked down.

A small, armed troop—five men on horseback—milled about in front of the closed portcullis, while a group of three, mounted and armed as well, waited off to the left.

"What is going on?" she asked Rolf. "Who are they? Are they all together?"

He shrugged. "I just got here myself, milady. But since they're not fighting each other, 'tis likely safe to assume they're at least on decent terms." He leaned out the window and shouted to the troops to identify themselves.

Before anyone could respond, Julianna peered past Rolf and caught sight of the banner, hanging limp in the still air, that one of the riders held. Her heart sank as the faint breeze lifted the pennon, exposing the dark outline of her uncle's heraldic device emblazoned on the triangle of fabric.

Damnation! "I believe 'tis my uncle," she muttered to Rolf before she leaned out the opening. "Raise the portcullis and open the gate for Lord Phillip d'Arcy," she shouted.

Her pulse raced; Uncle Phillip must have come

to take command of Tuck's Tower. It was her worst nightmare brought to life, and her sleep-muddled brain could see no way out of the situation.

Certainly nothing she could implement in the brief time before her uncle and his party rode in.

She'd never been craven in her life, but at the moment she wished she could hide, run away—do something, anything to avoid the upcoming confrontation. For what other reason would her uncle have bestirred himself to come here, even riding through the night?

Frustration made her want to stomp her feet, to thrust her sword repeatedly into the most heinous villain imaginable, to scream in sheer dissatisfaction. She had no doubt her life was about to change, and she was powerless to stop it.

Yet buried deep beneath that reaction was the silent acknowledgement that 'twould be a relief to have help, at least, to shoulder her duties.

She refused to contemplate exactly what that might mean, however.

Instead Julianna squared her shoulders, tossed her hair back out of her way, and descended to the bailey to welcome her uncle to Tuck's Tower.

By the time she reached the bailey, people had

begun to wander out of the barracks and the keep, scurrying about to prepare for the unexpected visitors. By the time her uncle and his men rode into the courtyard and dismounted, Julianna and a small group of servants and stable hands awaited them.

Schooling her face to show nothing but pleasure at her uncle's arrival—and despite her concerns, she *was* happy to see him—Julianna approached him, hands outstretched, and returned his embrace. "Welcome, Uncle. 'Tis good to see you." His resemblance to her father brought a momentary pang of sadness to her heart, swiftly defeated by the affection she felt for him. "I trust you are well. I wasn't aware you were coming, else we'd be better prepared for your visit. I trust nothing is wrong?"

Her hands held firm in his, her uncle stepped back a pace and scanned her face in the everbrightening light, his own expression a mixture of curiosity and concern. "Perhaps I should be asking *you* if something is wrong, Julianna. I don't believe I've ever heard you babble before today. Truly, you don't sound yourself."

Without waiting for a reply, he turned and gave

quiet orders to his men, then began to lead Julianna toward the keep.

She halted and turned to scan the bailey. "Where are your other men, Uncle?"

"I had no others, Julianna. There are five of us—"

"There were three men waiting outside, beyond the gatehouse," she told him. She hurried back toward the gatehouse, her uncle hard on her heels.

"Rolf!" she called up the stairwell. Despite trying to keep her tone even, calm, she could hear a trace of panic there. "Is that other group still out there?"

"Julianna, wait." Her uncle laid a hand on her arm. "Be easy, child—I believe they're yours." He nodded toward the men already riding through the gateway.

Julianna's breath shuddered from her chest, leaving her knees weak and her emotions unsteady. She hadn't even considered…to have been so careless….

Perhaps 'twould be best if Uncle Phillip *did* take her away with him and put someone else in command of Tuck's Tower, for her wits had surely gone lacking of late.

Right around the same time Will Bowman entered her life, a sly voice murmured in her mind.

Mayhap she was more woman than warrior after all, too easily distracted by a handsome man.

"'Tis Sir William,'' Rolf called down to her.

The news lifted her heart with relief—that he'd returned safely, and that he *had* come back as he'd said he would.

It also left her shaken, for what if her uncle took one look at her and Will and knew what they'd done?

She was a woman grown, Julianna reminded herself. She commanded troops, managed a keep... If she chose to share her body with a man, 'twas her own concern, no one else's.

Except if she got herself with child, or brought shame to the family name....

Uncle Phillip caught her by the arm and turned her to face him. "Julianna, are you unwell?" he asked kindly. "I realize I likely dragged you from your bed, but I've never seen you look so pale and distracted.''

"I'm fine, sir, truly.'' *Only a bit panic-stricken, for too many reasons I don't wish to share.*

"Lady Julianna.'' Will spoke from behind her, his tone formal.

She turned to face him, careful not to reveal her pleasure. "Welcome back, Sir William."

He bowed respectfully, his expression polite.

"Uncle, may I introduce Sir William Bowman—"

"Close the gates at once!" someone shouted, interrupting her. The ear-splitting squeal and thud of the portcullis dropping to place was followed by a commotion outside the curtain wall.

Rolf raced out of the stairwell, barely remaining on his feet in his haste. "'Tis Belleville, milady, with an army."

Bedlam erupted around them as servants and men-at-arms, animals and children all seemed to appear in the bailey at one time.

Julianna gathered up her hair and, tugging a leather thong off her sword hilt, bound it out of her way. Swords drawn, they headed for the stairs to the curtain wall. "Where did they come from?" she asked. "Uncle, Will—you were both just out there. How did they manage to conceal themselves from you?"

She didn't expect an answer, though the question echoed in her mind.

Julianna, her uncle, Will and Rolf gained the best vantage point on the wall and stood there gazing out at the mass of men arrayed before the front gates.

"'Tis Belleville," Rolf confirmed. "Though whether I'd call that an army, or a large troop, is questionable."

Julianna rolled her eyes at Rolf's weak attempt at humor. "There are enough of them to cause us grief," she pointed out. "Though they don't appear very eager to fight."

Indeed, few of the soldiers even had their weapons drawn and ready to use.

"What is this, then?" Julianna asked. Her temper stirred, she paced along the wall, seeking some sight of Belleville among his men.

She finally found him, seated on a large black destrier, hovering behind the dubious protection of a battering ram.

"Belleville!" she shouted. She waited until he nudged his mount into motion and moved nearer the front of his troops.

Will had followed her; he took her by the arm. "Let me, love," he murmured.

Julianna shook her head and shrugged free of his loose hold. "Sir Richard, what is the meaning of this ridiculous display? Do you believe you can frighten me into submission by simply bringing fighters to my gates?'' She rested her elbows on the top of the wall, making certain he could see her sword. ''You insult me! Begone at once, or prepare for war.''

Will touched her arm again. ''I don't believe his men want to fight. Lord Rannulf would never stand for this kind of poaching of a neighbor's lands, and Belleville's men know it. Perhaps if we—''

''Julianna,'' Belleville called. He sat strangely in the saddle, leaning a bit to one side as though he favored his ribs.

''I never gave that bastard leave to use my name,'' she snarled, her temper rising higher.

''We can come to terms without bloodshed, don't you think?'' Belleville asked. ''Give me control of Tuck's Tower, and hand over my sister Rachel, and I will even consider wedding you so you may remain here. We could command Tuck's Tower and Birkland together,'' he added with an unctuous smile.

Chaos erupted around her as Will, her uncle and Rachel—who had suddenly appeared nearby—all began shouting various forms of abuse at Belleville in response to his outrageous suggestions.

Belleville's men, by contrast, stood silently waiting, offering their leader no support in word or deed.

He, however, appeared quite oblivious to either reaction.

Or to the fact that the villagers who lived outside the confines of Tuck's Tower—nearly all retired members of Robin's band or their descendents—had armed themselves and crept up behind Belleville's troops, holding them confined between the castle wall and their own numbers.

She faced Will. "Has he run mad? I don't understand how he believes he can prevail."

Turning back toward Belleville, she peered more closely at him. Even at this distance she could see the sweat pouring down his face and his ashen color. "Is he ill?"

"He looks it," Will agreed. "Perhaps that would explain why he's here."

"Whatever the reason, he couldn't have chosen a worse time," she muttered.

"Is there ever a good time for this?" Will asked.

"Some are better than others," she pointed out with a glance over her shoulder at her uncle.

She returned her attention to the men outside.

"Sir Richard," she shouted. "I believe you are unwell. If you'll surrender your weapons, you may leave unharmed."

That statement caused another burst of shouting all around.

Belleville ignored it all and, raising his sword high, roared his battle cry at the top of his lungs. Before he could spur his mount into motion, however, he slumped over his horse.

His sword fell to the ground; his body followed. One of his men ran to him, felt his neck, and stepped back, making the sign of the cross and shaking his head.

Sir Richard Belleville, a gush of his blood staining the earth he'd coveted, was dead.

Belleville's troops laid down their weapons and surrendered straightaway. Once Julianna recovered from her shock, she sprang into action. As soon as she'd sent some of her men-at-arms out to recover Sir Richard's body and deal with his army, she asked her uncle, Will, Rachel and Rolf to join her inside the keep.

After sending for wine and food, Julianna shut the door to the anteroom off the great hall and leaned back against the wall for a moment, yearning for more time to gather her thoughts.

"Julianna." Her uncle's voice brought a swift end to that futile wish. Glancing up, she saw that he stood behind the chair at the head of the table. He gestured for her to take it. "Come, sit."

Surprised, Julianna glanced at the others, who stood by the benches along either side of the table—waiting for her to sit down, evidently. Masking her uncertainty, she removed her sword belt and took the seat.

Reining in her spinning brain, she decided to resume where she'd been interrupted earlier. "Uncle, may I introduce Rachel Belleville, Sir Richard's sister? Rolf you know," she added. "And Sir William Bowman, a knight in the service of Lord Rannulf FitzClifford, overlord of Birkland." Her uncle met each person's gaze with a searching look and a nod of greeting. "This is Lord Phillip d'Arcy, my overlord."

Will returned Lord Phillip's stare, his own gaze even. He knew this man was important to Julianna. From what little he'd observed thus far, her uncle respected her, as well as held a deep affection for her, both of which boded well for Julianna's future at Tuck's Tower.

And boded ill, perhaps, for Will's own chance of a future with Julianna.

A knock at the door heralded a maidservant carrying a tray of food and drink. Julianna waited until the woman served them and left before she spoke again.

"Uncle, what brought you here now?" she asked outright.

Lord Phillip raised an eyebrow. "Can I not visit my niece?"

"As much as I know you love me, 'twould not have brought you here traveling through the night," she pointed out.

"True," he agreed, amusement in his eyes. "But 'tis my affection and concern for you that brought me here—at the earl of Pembroke's behest."

"Pembroke? He knows nothing of me," she said.

"No—but he does know Sir William." Lord Phillip smiled and turned to Will. "He thinks quite highly of you, and trusts you to know what you're doing. He knew I was in Lincoln. As soon as he heard what you had to say about Belleville, about Julianna and Tuck's Tower, as well as recent events—" he added with a glance from Will to Julianna "—he sent word that you needed me here."

Recalling some of the issues he'd discussed with Pembroke, Will had to wonder precisely what Pembroke told d'Arcy. 'Twas enough to make him want to squirm beneath d'Arcy's measuring gaze, for he knew he'd said enough about Julianna to reveal his growing feelings toward her.

"Sir Richard did us a favor by dropping dead so conveniently," d'Arcy said wryly. "My apologies, Mistress," he said to Rachel. "And my condolences."

"Uncle!" Julianna cried, though to Will, she didn't sound truly upset.

Rachel didn't appear to mourn her brother's death, either. "He will pay for his sins now, I'm sure," was all she said.

Lord Phillip shrugged. "Pembroke wanted me to remove him from his position at Birkland. Since he was unlikely to have left quietly, his unexpected death serves us well, don't you think?"

'Twas certainly convenient, though there hadn't been time for Pembroke or d'Arcy to have aided Belleville on his way. "I wonder how he died?" Will asked.

"I'm sure we'll learn that in time," d'Arcy

said. "In the meantime, however, I'd rather get Julianna settled."

Julianna's cheeks went pale; did she fear what her uncle might do to her? Will had already seen enough to realize the man held Julianna in high regard.

She stood and braced her hands on the table. "If you plan to send me away from Tuck's Tower, Uncle, just tell me now."

"Why ever would I want to do that?" he asked, sounding amazed by her words. "Sit, child, and cease your worrying."

She did as her uncle bid her, though she still appeared concerned.

"I wish to reinforce my faith in you, Julianna. You've been a fine commander for Tuck's Tower, and I'm certain you will continue to be so, no matter what the future holds for you," he added with a glance at Will.

Julianna smiled. "Thank you, milord. I'll try to justify your faith in me."

Lord Phillip turned to Will. "As for you, Sir William—Pembroke wishes you to assume command of Birkland. He's already sent word to FitzClifford. I'm sure you'll hear from him soon to confirm the matter.'' He stood and held out his hand to Will. ''Congratulations.''

Will stood and shook d'Arcy's hand in a daze. His own command—and better yet, a property abutting Julianna's own.

He sent d'Arcy a questioning look. The older man merely smiled.

As Will accepted good wishes and talk turned to the defense of both holdings, Will's gaze kept drifting to Julianna.

Soon, he told himself—soon they'd settle *their* future, as well.

Chapter Twenty-Four

Sherwood Forest, near Tuck's Tower

"Come along, Will." Julianna tugged on Will's hand and drew him along the worn, narrow path. The deeper they traveled into the forest, the more muted the daylight became, until it bore a greenish tinge from the canopy of leaves overhead. She didn't need much light to find her way, however, for she'd walked this path a thousand times before. "You'll like this, I promise you."

She stopped beside a small dam, letting the sound of the water soothe her. 'Twas just what she needed after the chaos and death of recent days. Since her uncle's arrival and Sir Richard's death, there had scarce been a moment when she and Will weren't surrounded by other people, faced with the countless demands of bringing life back to normal at Tuck's Tower.

Finally, in desperation she and Will had stolen away and sought peace and privacy within the depths of Sherwood Forest.

She slipped her arms around Will's waist and rested her head on his shoulder. "This is my favorite place," she said. "If the stream wasn't so muddy I'd tear off your clothes and push you into the water."

"That sounds promising," he whispered into her hair. "What does a bit of mud matter?"

"You'd care if the creatures in the muck started biting your tender parts." She laughed, tightening her arms for a moment, then stepped away. "Come. This is nearly as good." She drew him deeper into the forest.

An ancient oak grew near the stream, its branches full and sturdy. "My father built this for me when I was small. 'Twas so I could imagine I lived in Sherwood. He wanted me to know something of my other father."

She scanned the overgrown underbrush. "We pretended to be Robin of the Hood and the Black Knight, right here in the forest." She wove her fingers with his. "You played those same games as a child, didn't you? You talked about it when you had a fever."

"Aye, Gillian and I, and the other children at l'Eau Clair." He released her hand and gave her unbound hair a tug. "I'll wager you were not Maid Marian, were you?" he asked, chuckling.

She shook her head. "Nay—I always wanted to be the Black Knight."

"It amazes me still, milady, knowing that you carry the blood of my childhood heroes within you." Will stared up into the oak. "Shall we play together now?" he asked, his tone a teasing invitation.

Julianna suppressed a shiver of reaction and smiled; she was more than ready to play any games Will might suggest.

Reaching up, she found the rope ladder hanging from the trunk and tugged it down. "Here you go." She held out the ladder. "There are eight rungs."

"Is it safe, or am I going to get halfway up and fall on my arse?" he asked. "That doesn't sound romantic to me."

"Imagine all the things I could do to you while

you were forced to lie abed," she teased. "It will hold, but if you don't believe me, I'll go first."

Will stepped back out of her way and gestured for her to go ahead. "I look forward to it," he said with a meaningful glance at her long skirts.

Sending him a challenging look of her own, Julianna slowly kilted up her gown, purposely exposing her legs to above her knees, and scrambled up the rungs. "I should have started wearing lady's garb sooner," she called down as she waited for Will.

"I'm glad you started now," he said once he joined her.

She unrolled the tattered leather curtain that hung over the doorway, surrounding them in a soft darkness. Working by feel, she rolled up the canvas window covers and located the lantern beside the door. Soon a mellow glow filled the small dwelling.

It hadn't changed much over the years, other than the pallet she'd added when she was fifteen and came here to hide away and dream. Back then she'd have been horrified to imagine sharing that bed with a man. Now she could scarcely wait.

She sat on the straw mattress and lounged back.

"Care to join me?" she asked, patting the spot beside her.

Will leaned against the trunk of the tree and smiled lazily. "Depends on what you've got in mind."

She sent him a seductive look, slipped off her shoes and brought her legs up onto the bed. She slid her gown high along on her thighs, until the tops of her stockings were almost exposed.

Her heart started to thump harder as he pushed away from the tree and walked to the bed. Dropping to his knees beside the bed, he laid his hand on the hem of her gown. "Anyone nearby that I should know about?" he murmured. "Or are we alone?"

"Alone." Taking a deep breath, she tried to get her bearings. His hand seemed to burn through her gown, heating her blood and stirring her imagination.

"There'd better not be anyone in the area," he said. "Because I think we might be noisy."

"Good." Feeling bold, she pressed her mouth to his and dragged her tongue along the line of his lips. His groan spurred her to reach for the ties of his shirt, teasing him with her mouth while she slowly unknotted the strings.

Will hadn't moved his hand, but his fingers curled around her thigh, branding her with his touch. She wanted more, but felt a bit shy about asking for it. Instead she pushed the neck of his shirt open and pressed her palms to his flesh.

His leanly muscled chest rose and fell in reaction to her touch, luring her to run her fingertips through the dark curls on his chest and scraping her nails over his skin.

He tore his mouth from hers and rested his cheek against hers. "God, Julianna—you make me wild. My mind says to go slow, but instead I want to grab you. What do you want?"

"After the way you teased me when we made love before, I think 'tis my turn to torment *you*."

"Who was teasing?" he asked. "You've been teasing me from the moment we left the keep today. Knowing that this—" he moved her skirts up her leg, exposing her stocking and her naked thigh "—was right there under your gown drove me wild. I wanted to do this—" he hooked his finger in her garter "—and this." Leaning down, he drew his tongue over the flesh above the stocking.

When he bit lightly at her thigh, Julianna thought she'd melt right there. She'd never thought of such things till she met Will. She groaned and fell back among the pillows. "You're making my head spin," she groaned.

"Good. What are you thinking?" Slowly dragging her skirts up, Will slid his fingers into the top of the stocking and slid it down her leg, his mouth spreading heat in its wake. After he tugged it off her foot, he moved to the other leg and repeated the process.

He expected her to think? Julianna could scarcely do more than feel and react to the fire in his touch. She needed to kiss him, craved his lips on hers and his hands everywhere.

Burying her fingers in his hair, she pulled him up onto the bed with her and shoved his shirt over his shoulders, yanking it free of his braes and tossing it aside.

Her hands didn't falter this time when she undid his belt and untied his braes. Unable to resist, she drew her nails through the hair on his stomach, the hiss of his indrawn breath goading her on.

"Wait," he muttered. He reached down and jerked his boots off, then wriggled out of his leggings. He stretched out beside her and stared into her eyes. "I think you're wearing too many clothes. I'd better do something about that.'' He stripped off her gown and undertunic in record time, then bent to kiss her nipples through the sheer silk of her chemise.

"You taste so sweet," he said, nuzzling the valley between her breasts.

With all her attention focused on Will's lips, she didn't notice he'd begun to slide up her chemise until she felt the cool night air on her stomach, followed by the heat of his palm. The contrast was enticing, especially when combined with his touch on her breasts.

Sighing, Julianna lay back and savored the onslaught of sensation.

Even the brush of Julianna's warm skin against him made his aching flesh burn with need. He wanted to slow down, but his body urged him to take Julianna, to make her his without delay. He felt sparks flow through his blood, spurred on by the beautiful woman spread out before him like a feast—for his eyes, his hands, his senses.

Julianna had been right, there was something seductive, romantic, about the murmur of flowing water, the soft glow of her flesh in the faint light of the lantern.

He brushed his lips over her as she lay within

his embrace—lips, breasts, stomach, the soft curls at the juncture of her thighs—anointing her with his love. He heard the word in his head without fanfare, without fear. It simply was. He loved Julianna d'Arcy, loved the things she gave him, the way she made him feel. A different Will Bowman existed because of her, a man less driven, more content to savor life.

He felt worthy.

Worthy of anything, including her love if she chose to give it to him. God, he hoped she did.

She stirred beneath his touch, her body seeking his in an unmistakable way. But he wasn't yet ready to give in to the passion driving through him. He wanted to make her want—no, need—him as much as he needed her.

By the time he had Julianna writhing on the pallet, he thought he might explode from wanting her. He kissed his way up her body, taking her mouth in a driving kiss that was a weak substitute for what he truly wanted.

"Will," she pleaded, her voice husky with desire. "Don't make me wait any longer." Her hands shook as she cradled him in her hands.

Now he *knew* he'd explode if he couldn't make her his soon. Her fingertips stroked a path of fire, all around where he needed her touch the most, tempting him to grab her hand and move it.

But he didn't. After the way he'd teased her, he owed her the same courtesy. After all, 'twas a contest neither would lose.

He reached the point where he couldn't take any more of her sweet torture without giving in to the driving need to explode with pleasure. He wanted to be inside her for that.

Lips fused to hers, he caught her hands in his and drew them away from his aching flesh. "Love, I'll never last if you touch me now."

She rose up to meet him as he slipped into her warmth, wrapping her legs around him as though she'd never let go. Holding him tightly with arms and legs, she moved with him, until they fell into passion together.

Julianna drifted up from the depths of passion, her mind no more ready than her body to return to the world outside. Will lay snuggled against her; the pallet was a tight fit, especially for two tall people. But she didn't mind. There was no place she'd rather be than in his arms.

She heard him murmur something into her hair, but she couldn't understand the words. "What did you say?" she asked, her voice sleepy.

He burrowed into her tangled tresses, drew her closer and mumbled again.

"Will, I can't hear you." She slid her head away from him, forcing him to move off her hair.

Sighing, he raised his head and stared into her eyes. Something within his warm gaze called to her, but she didn't know what it was. He swept her hair back from her face and touched her cheek. "I said, I love you."

Julianna had heard people say their heart skipped a beat, but she'd always assumed 'twas simply something people said, not an accurate description.

Now she knew 'twas true.

She didn't know what to say in response. Will had caused her to be, for one of the few times in her life, completely speechless. However, he couldn't mistake the meaning of the single tear running down her cheek.

Could he?

He looked uncertain, an unusual expression for him. She fought the tightness in her throat, sought some way to ease it so she could speak the words she thought he waited to hear.

Pinning him with her gaze, Julianna tried to put

her love into that look as she stroked his face and mouthed the words.

"Do you? Are you sure?" He looked like he wanted to believe her, but didn't quite dare.

She nodded.

"You're not saying it because I—"

"Nay," she whispered. Clearing her throat, she tried again. "I love you, as well, Will."

He crushed her to him. She couldn't mistake the need in that embrace, a need for far more than physical satisfaction.

"I know we haven't known each other very long, but the time we've spent together has been—intense, you could say." He pulled back and stared into her face. "You make me feel things I didn't think I knew how to feel. I like being with you, even when we're not in bed," he said with a laugh.

Julianna framed his face with her hands. "I do love you, Will. But do you think we need more time? Time to know each other better?" Though she couldn't imagine needing more time to know Will Bowman. She'd realized almost from their first meeting that there was an almost magical pull that drew them together.

"I'm glad we didn't take some things slow."

His gaze swept over her in a caress that sent a wave of heat over her. Will pressed his lips to hers in a kiss that was a promise of pleasure to come, as well as a vow. "I think that a lifetime might possibly give us time enough to know each other better."

Tears welled in Julianna's eyes.

Will cradled her head in his hands and smoothed her hair away from her face. "Nay, love, don't cry." He brushed his mouth across her brow. "I can wait—"

She shook her head. "No waiting," she whispered. She took a deep breath, drawing in strength and determination along with it once she looked deep into Will's eyes. "You won't escape me so easily, Will Bowman. I carried you off to my keep over my saddlebow. In my estimation, that means you're already mine," she told him. "You shan't elude me by waiting, or leaving, or any other excuse."

His lips curved in a smile, Will cradled Julianna close. "How could I fight so fierce a warrior?"

"You cannot. The Bride of the Tower has chosen her mate—if you'll have me as your wife."

His blue eyes aglow, Will took her hand in his,

pressed a kiss into her palm and pressed it over
his thundering heart. "Then your grateful captive—" he grinned "—is most pleased to accept
your offer, milady."

He bent close, his lips up against her ear. "The
next time though, love, may I carry you instead?"

* * * * *

SHARON SCHULZE

began writing romances while pursuing her first career as a civil engineer, and discovered that confirmed daydreamer/bookaholics can practice their craft anywhere, even someplace as unromantic as a wastewater treatment plant. In her writing, she gets the chance to experience days gone by—without encountering disease, vermin and archaic plumbing!

A New Hampshire native, she now makes her home in Connecticut with her husband, Cliff, their children, Patrick and Christina, and her "lovely assistant"—Samantha, a miniature dachshund. In her ever-shrinking spare time she enjoys movies, music and poking around in antique shops.

Readers may contact her at P.O. Box 180, Oakville, CT 06779.